SMUT

CENTRAL

A NOVEL BY
BRANDON McCALLA

smut
CENTRAL

WHERE
HIP HOP
LITERATURE
BEGINS...

AUGUSTUS
PUBLISHING

© 2010 Brandon McCalla
ISBN: 9780982541586

Novel by Brandon McCalla
Edited by Anthony Whyte
Creative Direction & Photography by Jason Claiborne

Augustus Publishing paperback June 2010
www.augustuspublishing.com

"Only enemies speak the truth; friends and lovers lie endlessly, caught in the web of duty."   — Stephen King

"A bad review is like baking a cake with all the best ingredients and having someone sit on it."   — Danielle Steel

ACKNOWLEDGEMENTS

I would like to thank Endria Chachere for the much needed editing help, love you so much. Vince McMahon has the best doctors!!! Special shout out to all the AKA ladies I know and haven't been formally introduced to- the green and the pink. You dames bless the earth with grace, beauty and elegance.

Charlene Braithwaite-Lovett, Naomi Gonzalez Howard, Arlene Ponce, Deesha Hutchins, La Jill Hunt, Desha Newman-Colon, Delonya Conyers and those I forgot to mention (sorry, my brain be bad sometimes), thanks for reading Smut Central early and letting me know what you felt. I'm very glad you reading vixens enjoyed. I see you Yoshe!!! I love my mommy...

Uno,
Brandon McCalla

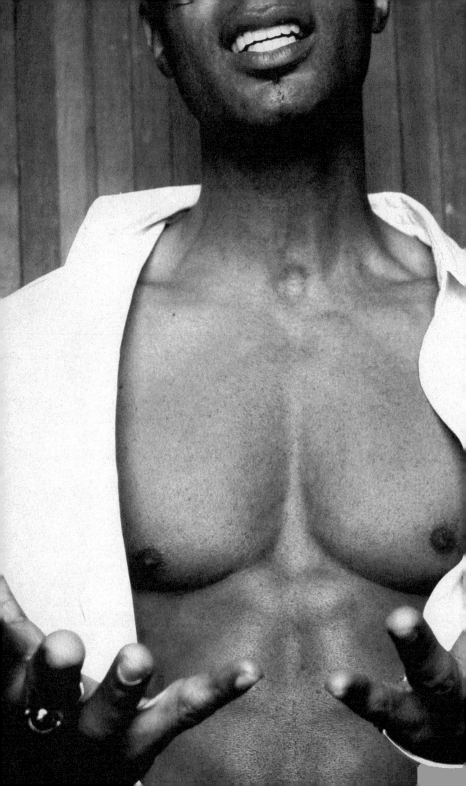

smut

CENTRAL

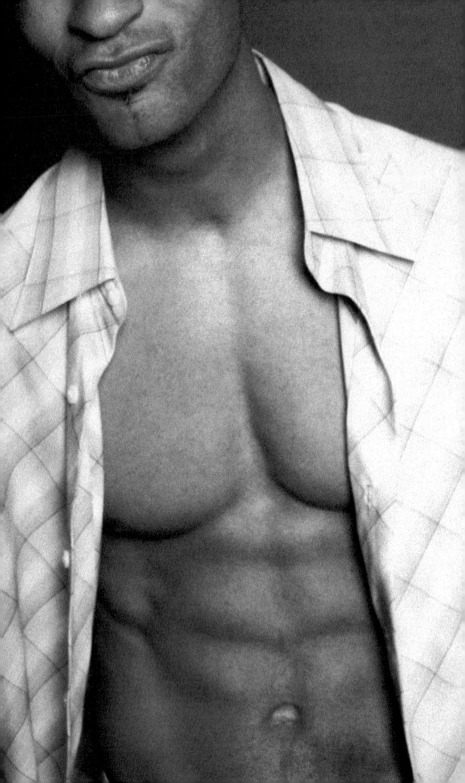

01

"Markus Johnson," the psychiatrist said, after he walked into her well furnished office. "Please, have a seat."

She waved an arm toward a long soft leather couch then she closed the door. Before sitting down, Markus walked over to a huge bookshelf, scrolled a finger over a couple of the leather bound text books. Most of the books on the shelf were school books from her college days. He laughed while looking at all the books on psychiatry and psychology she had studied. Eventually Markus sat down on the couch. The doctor sat on an adjacent chair facing the couch.

The psychiatrist crossed her long legs. She seemed to be in her early thirties, or maybe her well preserved forties. Her face was plain and she wore glasses, but there was an attraction.

It was her eyes, very dark blue and almond shaped. White stockings sheathed her toned legs. She had nicely defined hips, and thick thighs.

Slowly Markus's feet tapped softly against the rug as he eyed her body for a long while. He saw the way her eyes widened then narrowed. She wore a light brown, very conservative skirt suit, with white shirt. The heels she wore were modest, but the style spelled expensive.

Although her skirt hadn't pushed high enough for him to see whether she was wearing a garter or not, his imagination did the rest. She had a very sexy body. Her breasts were at least a thirty eight C cup. Markus wasn't sure what her ass looked like, but he was certain it looked as fuck-able as the rest of her body. He could tell she was used to men looking at her body. He finally stopped ogling her, and looked at her face.

"My daughter's mother recommended you. She said you might be able to help me, if you get my meaning."

Markus had decided to grab the bull by the horns, and take control of the first session. He wasn't completely sure why he was in a psychiatrist's office to begin with, but here he was on the couch nonetheless.

"Yes, Gwyneth, she told me you've been having anxiety attacks and you have been blacking out. You might have possibly been experiencing panic attacks. What did your primary doctor say?" The psychiatrist asked, eyeing him keenly.

"All the blood work and the neurological tests came back negative. Anxiety attacks…?" Markus scoffed. "Is that what she told you?"

"Yes, that is what Gwyneth shared with me," the psychiatrist readily smiled.

She was a bit perplexed when the tall handsome and well built Black man walked into her office. Her patient, Gwyneth was white, conservative, and very successful. This man was far younger than Gwyneth. He was wearing jeans, construction boots and a basketball jersey.

His thick platinum chain and the two rings on his right hand that twinkled with lots of diamonds appeared expensive. He looked like a rap star, a gangster or a drug dealer. Gwyneth told her he was famous, but never got into what sort of fame. She said he was harmless. Dr. Nancy Adler took a deep breath.

"Anxiety," Markus said, grimacing. "I don't know, but I have been blacking out," he said, staring suspiciously at her. "I blacked out in a club, in the middle of work another time, and once while I was just brushing my teeth."

Nancy Adler was a very well established shrink. Markus hadn't seen another Black person while he was in the waiting room. And from the way the secretary and the other patients were looking at him, none of them had seen any until he walked in the door.

"How old are you?" Dr. Adler asked.

She knew Gwyneth was in her late thirties, like she was. This man sitting on her couch couldn't be any older than twenty. He was a very impressively built man, not too muscular, but tall. Nancy Adler could see why a woman like Gwyneth would be sexually attracted to him. She had gotten pregnant by him, and they had a daughter together.

"Why do you ask?"

"Why wouldn't I?" Dr. Adler replied.

"Cute," he said with a snicker. "That rebuttal was cute. Did one of those books on that shelf teach you that?"

"As a matter of fact, yes one did," Dr. Adler smiled, even though she knew he was trying to get under her skin. "I would guess you are, a year or two older or younger than twenty-one."

"True," Markus answered. "I'm around that. Why do you ask?" before she could reply, he said, "Is it the age difference between Gwyneth and myself or…?" Markus asked, tracing both index fingers down the sides of his defined torso. "Is it this, if you get my meaning…"

Markus waited for a reaction, but the psychiatrist paused coolly before responding.

"Gwyneth hasn't spoken much about you. Quite frankly, I didn't expect to see what I saw when you walked in."

"No one in the waiting room did either. Shit, Doctor, I don't wanna be here, Gwyneth recommended you. She said you're her shrink. And that my anxiety attacks, blackouts or whatever, might be psychological, if you get my meaning?"

"They may well be, Mr. Johnson."

"Call me Markus, or Mr. Excitement, that's what everybody calls me, Mr. Excitement."

"Mr. Excitement…?" She repeated sarcastically. "Are you some sort of celebrity, a rapper, perhaps…?" Dr. Adler paused smirking. "Maybe you're an athlete… A basketball player…?"

"None of the above," he said with a sardonic smile. "I'm an adult entertainer."

"Excuse me…?" She exclaimed. "An adult entertainer…?"

"Yeah, a porn star if you get my meaning? You don't watch porn?"

"I haven't seen one in a very long time."

"I'll make sure you get a couple copies of my flicks. They're very popular," Markus proudly laughed. "I'm a very good performer."

"Ahem, you said you blacked out during work. Was it during…?" Dr. Adler asked, looking uncomfortable.

"Kind of… If you get my meaning," he uttered.

"And you also blacked out while you were brushing your teeth. What were you thinking about during these two incidents… ah activities…?"

"Hmm," Markus mused for a beat. "I was thinking about how beautiful the girl was. She had the nicest ass. See, she was what we call a newbie in the biz, a virgin to the camera. I was breaking her in. Her name is Vonchell, I think. Yeah, it was Vonchell, the up and cumin' porn diva. She's the best-looking vixen I've been with on film," he said reflectively. "That girl was a little shy at first. So I was loosening her up, if you get my meaning. We were doing an awesome oral scene, and I just blacked out."

"I see," Dr. Adler worded dryly. "Continue…"

"She was on her fours. That's industry talk for doggie style, if you get my meaning…" Markus winked mischievously.

"Okay…" The doctor said, listening intently. She was not amused.

"I was in front of her. She had just finished polishing me off. That's industry talk for…" He continued.

"I think I get it Mr. Johnson…"

"Please Doctor, call me Markus," he paused, smiling before continuing. "In any event, I moved behind her. We finished with the oral, and was about to get the vaginal penetration on camera, from behind. There was no need for any cut and redirection. Our scenes were all great. The chemistry we had was good."

"It all sounds so technical," she uttered with sarcasm under her breath.

"It is, if you get my meaning…?" he responded sarcastically. "I had my dick in my hand, jerking off. Then I was about to push in-between them perfect ass cheeks…"

"Oh!" the psychiatrist blurted with widened eyes.

Markus saw her cheeks glowing red. He smiled. "All of a sudden, I started getting flashbacks of my past, I think. Bits and pieces, I can't remember. Then I just blacked out."

"What about your past?" She asked. "And the bits and pieces you can't remember, what exactly do you mean?"

"I can only recall as far back as when I was eight or nine years old. Then sometimes I see things… Images, people, places, my parents I think and, and…" Markus wanted to say more, but couldn't speak.

It was like there was no air in the room. He couldn't breathe. *He saw a man and a woman. They were waving at him, looking at him with fake smiles on their faces. He saw a little girl with them. She was crying. Someone was dragging him away…Away from them, away from his family…*

The room began spinning and all the oxygen was sucked out of it. He thought he heard the psychiatrist ask him, "Are you okay?" He thought he heard her say, "Quickly, lie back down on the couch."

He didn't realize he was rising from his sitting position until his legs turned to jelly. He fell back down on the couch. Everything suddenly went dark.

02

"Drink this," Dr. Adler said to the recently revived Markus Johnson.

He was lying on the couch, looking at the plain faced psychiatrist who was looking down at him. In her hand, she had a glass of water. Markus got into a sitting position before graciously accepting the glass.

After he took a couple of gulps, he asked, "How long was I in La-La-Land?"

"La-La-Land...?" She snickered at what he named his blackouts. "Only for a couple of minutes, I was able to revive you with smelling salt. I always have a bottle handy for this sort of occasion, Mr. Johnson." She sat back in a chair facing the couch. "How long are you usually out during these blackouts, without being revived?"

"I don't know, maybe an hour or so." Markus saw the doctor's expression and asked, "Is that bad?"

"Blackouts are not good all by themselves, regardless of how long or short you are unconscious. You just lie in slumber. Some people have been known to function during blackouts. And that can be dangerous."

"What do you mean by function?"

"Like sleep walking, you were about to say something about your parents. I asked you what you were thinking of during one of your blackouts. And you said you were thinking about your past. How do you feel now? Do you feel like you are going to go back to," she asked smirking, "La-La-Land?"

"No," he answered. "Gwyneth didn't tell you much about me?"

"No," she said. Then she smiled at Markus. "Gwyneth as you well know has problems of her own. You never seemed to be one of them."

"Okay, that's true."

"Now about the bits and pieces of your past and you only being able to remember as far back as nine years old? You are so young? You should be able to remember more, much more?"

"I don't know what it is," he replied honestly. "It's like I woke one day in the middle of my life. I was around eight or nine years old, in an orphanage. I stayed there till I was about fourteen. Then I ran away. I was homeless, out on the streets of New York, bouncing from shelter to shelter, doing what I had to do to survive for about ten months. I met Gwyneth, and she took me away from all that."

"My God...!" She exclaimed.

The psychiatrist didn't know what else to say. She couldn't fathom a woman like Gwyneth Manners harboring the young Black teenager from off the streets. "Are you telling me you awoke one day in an orphanage, not knowing how you got there, and no recollection of what actually happened?"

"Yes, I mean no. See, I knew my name but other than that, nothing else. The people at the orphanage told me I fell and hit my head so hard I lost consciousness. And when I came to, I lost my memory. Don't look at me like that doctor, before you ask, no I don't know who my parents are. The people at the orphanage never told me a damn thing about myself. They said they had no information anyway. They said someone dropped me at the doorstep, rang the bell and ran off, if you get my meaning…"

"Astounding…!" She exclaimed.

"I think I see my parents before each blackout. There was the first time at the club, and then before the doggie style scene with Vonchell… Then it happened while I was brushing my teeth, and here on this couch. I don't know anything about my past. I didn't hang around the orphanage long enough to find out. The orphanage was bad news. Gwyneth took me to the social security office but there wasn't any record of me. I haven't a birth certificate either. It's like the beginning of my life up to that age was erased. It's like I wasn't even born, if you get my meaning…"

"I can't believe this?" Dr. Adler said with genuine bewilderment.

Before she could say anything else Markus said, "I didn't come here to talk about my past. I'm here to talk about my present, if you get my meaning… The anxiety attacks."

"I'm not sure if your blackouts are due to anxiety, though I believe you are suffering from something psychological. And you see things before you blackout. I find that interesting. The fact that there is no record of your birth and you not having a social security number is very unusual. Perhaps you are from another country."

"Like Africa, or somewhere like that, doctor? Perhaps," Markus mumbled.

He drained the glass of water and got off the couch. The

psychiatrist looked as if she would stand as well. Markus held a hand out motioning for her to remain seated. "Dr. Adler…"

"Call me Nancy, Mr. Excitement," she said.

"Call me Markus, Nancy. Mr. Excitement is a stage name. I wanna be real with you. What I tell you is no act. The place I be seeing before blacking out is an urban area. Like right here in New York City, somewhere, I think."

She watched him walk over to her desk. He placed the empty glass atop it. He reached for a book she had on the desk. "Sometimes, I read books and know the ending of the story before I reach the second chapter. Children's books, and no, I ain't dumb or nothing, but I'm very curious at times. I look at children's things to see if they'll trigger something in me. Gwyneth told me something might spark some of my memories. She was right. I once did a movie in Brazil, and I felt as if I was there before. It's like I know of places I've never been. I don't think about these things much, I hang out in the streets. And when its time to do a porno my agent calls me, and I go do the damn thing."

"You might have possibly read those books and been to these places, Markus. How can you be sure when you have no recollection of a great deal of your past?"

"True…"

"Let's talk about the first time you blacked out, and these bits and pieces of your past?" she asked.

Markus walked back to the couch and sat down. He began rubbing his bald head. Dr. Adler thought he might blackout again. He didn't. She gave him a concerned look. He looked at her, smiled and said, "The first time it happened was over a month ago, at this lounge. I met this woman. She's the most beautiful woman in the world. She didn't give me the time of day. She was with a few of her coworkers and friends. There was something about her. I couldn't stop looking. I was drawn to her. It was like I had seen her before, but I couldn't recall ever seeing or meeting her."

"Go on," the doctor ordered.

"I offered to buy her a drink, she refused. Something about her must have triggered something in my mind. I started seeing things, a building somewhere, two people who might be my parents. Then I just blacked out."

The psychiatrist said, "Interesting," After a brief silence between the two. "Tell me about the second incident?" she said.

"The second time was just before the doggie style scene with Vonchell. We were shooting the film in this huge hotel suite the entertainment company used a couple of times. I saw a little girl, of all things. And I saw those same people again. I was being yanked away by someone. Apparently I didn't want to go where that person was taking me. The little girl was crying. She was crying..."

"They might possibly be your parents and that little girl, a relation of some sort. What about the third time?"

"The third time was when I was in the bathroom brushing my teeth. I can't remember what I was thinking about. But when I blacked out; those two people and the little girl again, I always see the same thing before blacking out. Those were flashbacks, right?" He said looking at the doctor with uncertainty.

"Quite possibly so, I would believe that is what they are. You must describe them to me in greater detail, without blacking out this time," she smiled. "Listen, all of this might be beyond me. I know a good hypnotist who could..."

Markus waved his hand, cutting Nancy off in mid sentence. "No hypnotist. Gwyneth said whatever we discuss wouldn't go as far as the walls of your office. Let's just keep this between us."

"Everything we discuss is strictly confidential. And if you don't want a hypnotist, I understand. Hypnosis is often used to help people with amnesia. I thought maybe it could help your situation."

Markus's cellphone beeped. "One moment," he said to Nancy, getting off the couch. He walked to one of the windows.

Nancy had so many questions to ask. She was certain Markus had some record of his existence, somewhere. He was possibly having flashbacks of his past. Nancy was sure hypnosis could help. It would provide more help than she could. She needed to know more. Markus got off the phone. Instead of sitting back down he began walking toward the door.

"Where are you going?" She asked him.

"I gotta run. The session is over anyway, isn't it? It's been over a half hour ago."

She glanced at the clock on the wall, and said, "That is true, Markus. But I still have a few more questions I need to ask. I think with a little time, we can make some progress."

"I'm certain we could, but I gotta go." He was halfway out the door when he turned. "Is there any medication you can prescribe, something that will stop me from having these black outs, if you get my meaning…?"

"Maybe anxiety medication, Seredyn or Xanax may help. But I'm not sure if your blackouts are triggered from anxiety. I still need to conduct further examinations," she said with a touch of concern.

"You have me for three more sessions. One day a week. I guess I'll see you next week at the same time," he said then walked out.

The psychiatrist's curiosity was peaked as she watched him leave.

03

Markus walked out the psychiatrist's office. He hopped inside the car parked across the street, and called his agent back.

"Audra," he said when she answered the phone. "I can talk now, what's up?"

"You're up, or can you get it up," Audra laughed. Then her tone got serious. "What happened to you the other day? Why did you pass out? Are you okay?"

"The doctor said it was dehydration," he lied. "I feel much better. When are we gonna finish shooting this movie?"

"Tomorrow," she said sternly. "You are so lucky. Smut Central Entertainment was very close to dropping your ass. You are the only stud in the movie. They had no other man on the premise that could perform like you. That is the only reason why they rescheduled."

"Sorry." He didn't know what else to say. "Same place, same time…?"

"Yeah Markus, same place, same time…" Her tone of voice got worse. "These people rarely reschedule. If you weren't as hot as you are, and your movies weren't selling. They would have dropped you and I would have no choice but to dismiss you as a client. I don't have time for shit like this. Do you know how many men are out there waiting to fill your position?"

"Was that a question or statement?" He chuckled. "Relax, Audra. I won't pass out tomorrow. It'll never happen again. I promise. And think, the fact that they want me back to finish tells you they really want me."

"Maybe, but how exciting is a Mr. Excitement who faints the moment he's about to stick his dick in a woman's ass."

"A woman's vagina," he corrected. "It wasn't an anal scene."

"Very funny, remind me to laugh later. This is the highest paying gig I got you so far. And mind you, you are the only client I have of this sort."

"I know, I know," he snapped in irritation. "I'm your secret client. Shit, does any other porn star on earth have an agent besides me?"

"Was that a question or statement? Don't fuck things up tomorrow. And Markus, you aren't a porn star. You're an adult entertainer. Remember that and drink lots of fluids. I want you functional tomorrow. You fuck up with S.C.E and you'll be right back where I found you. Fucking those nasty rap video bitches for beer money…" Audra said, disconnecting the call.

"Shit," Markus blurted once he started the car engine. "I'm tired of fucking bitches for money anyway."

Markus hadn't many choices in life. Sex on camera had eventually become one. Gwyneth showed him affection, love, and gave him options. She didn't expose him to a world of lights, camera, and action, but she started him down the road. Coercing him to fulfill sexual fantasies for her and her friends, she started him down the path that he now willingly trudged. Slipping into swinger clubs with her friends, Markus eventually landed in the porn industry. By age seventeen he was fucking on camera. He made an easy choice in life and started doing porn since he was a minor.

Markus rarely dwelled on things for more than a few seconds. He had no past and wanted no part of history. His present was one day at a time. Tomorrow would be spent back at the hotel suite, fucking gorgeous women and ejaculating on cue. He was good at it, and Markus was qualified to do it.

He didn't feel like going home just yet. Markus felt an urge to call Gwyneth. He hadn't seen his daughter in a couple of days, was missing her dearly. Seeing his daughter always came with a cost. It came with a price he wasn't always willing to pay because it involved doing things he now got paid to do. His daughter was possibly the only thing on the planet he loved. The world was starting to look different to Markus. He had seen a glimpse of his past. Before he blacked out those times he envisioned people in his mind, unknown people on the outskirts of his consciousness. He was beginning to remember, but didn't understand.

It had caused him to pass out on the job, and that wasn't a good look. Smut Central Entertainment paid him big, and they were the biggest adult entertainment company on the east coast. Ironcally Smut Central was his meal ticket out of the hot sex business. He couldn't see himself doing fuck films forever. Markus figured after a few big-paying gigs, he could move on, maybe even go to college. He could become normal.

His thoughts shifted gear to Tanisha, his friend. She would

be home. He had called her before walking into that psych's office. Tanisha was the only women in his life he didn't feel obligated to fuck. But every time he was with her, they fucked. It was what Markus did. He decided to go see her.

Markus was more than halfway close to Tanisha's place. He thought about the woman he met at the club, that woman who refused the drink he offered her. She was the most beautiful woman in the world, the one who had been triggering his blackouts and flashbacks. She sucked the oxygen from the car's interior.

All of a sudden Markus began feeling lightheaded. He could see the red light ahead. It was eight in the evening and Markus had just driven across the Brooklyn Bridge with the light Monday evening traffic. He became frantic and desperately drove with shaking hands toward a safer place out of the middle lane.

He pressed his foot on the brake pedal too hard. The vehicle swerved recklessly, Markus knew he had to stop, and put the damn thing in park before he blacked out. The car skidded then halted in a herky-jerky manner behind a parked car. He bumped the back of the car hard enough to set off the car's alarm. Then Markus saw those two people and the little girl.

She was crying. Looking at him as the space between them grew further away. He was being dragged somewhere. Someone had a firm grasp upon one of his wrists...

Everything was getting blurry. Things eventually began to darken, darken. It faded to black. Markus could no longer hear the alarm.

His eyes slowly fluttered open, the clock on the dashboard

read ten-thirty-five. Over two hours had passed by while he was in La-La-Land.

"What the fuck!"Markus cursed under his breath.

If he hadn't managed to maneuver, and park the car as quickly as he did, things could have gone ugly. The blackouts were starting to become life threatening. Markus sat in the car for another hour. Slowly he backed off the car he bumped, and continued to drive to Tanisha's.

Why did thinking about that woman trigger the blackout, he thought? "Shit," Markus blurted aloud. "I feel light headed again." He felt like he was going back to La-La-Land. He didn't. Trying not to think about anything, Markus concentrated on the road. He managed to drive all the way to Tanisha's without any further incident. He found parking a half block from her apartment building. Jumping out, he jogged to the front door and pressed the buzzer.

The door beeped twice then electronically unlocked. He went inside, walked three flights then knocked on Tanisha's door. She immediately noticed his bloodshot eyes when she opened the door.

"Markus, you look terrible," she said before he could enter the apartment.

"I feel terrible. I blacked out twice today."

"Damn," she replied. "What did the shrink say?"

"I'll tell you all about it later. Do you have any alcohol?"

"Of course I do, I'm an alcoholic," she sassed before chuckling. "Sit down and relax. I'll make you a drink."

While she poured drinks for them, Markus sat in her living room with his head in his hands, stressed out. He was pretty hard to figure out at times. Tanisha knew a blow job or some hot steamy sex were good remedies. Markus was different because he fucked for a living, maybe all he needed was a strong drink. She handed him a glass filled with gin and tonic.

"I need to be inside you…"

She was shocked to hear him say that. She watched him drink. Tanisha drained what was left in her glass.

Dropping to her knees, she was at his feet. Tanisha took the empty glass he was holding and placed it on the floor. In a hot second, his belt was being unbuckled. Markus leaned his head back on the couch and closed his eyes. He thought about nothing but the sensation of Tanisha's thick lips wrapped around his monstrously large penis. He could hear the slurping sound she made while sucking.

04

Stripping was usually the gateway to the porn industry. Markus met Tanisha, a professional stripper a year ago at a porn shoot. She was one of the girls he had to fuck. It was her first time on film. Tanisha went from dancing semi-nude, to butt naked. She moved on to sucking dick in the VIP rooms then landed in sex on camera. Markus made sure her first sex scene was her last. He had blown her pussy out with his massive dick the day they met. Then he blew out another girl's vagina after he finished with Tanisha.

They went out to eat afterwards, the three of them. He dated many of the women he fucked on film, getting behind-the-scenes practice fucking them, and moving on to the next. He preferred women in the business because they were the only sort of woman who understood his line of work. There were not a lot of decent women who would stay with a guy who fucked various other women for a living.

Tanisha was different and they formed a close ally. Most other women were in his life for as long as it took him to bust off. Tanisha took Markus' advice the first day they met, and she never made another sex film. Stripping was how she paid her rent, but that was all she did. There were no more sucking off men in Champagne rooms. Gwyneth had his baby but Gwyneth was more a business arrangement than a woman of his. Tanisha was the closest to a girlfriend Markus had ever had.

She jerked his dick aggressively while bobbing her head up and down. Her soft mouth was working the upper shaft of his hugeness with vigor. She gagged on him four or five times during deep throat attempts. His huge girth caused her mouth and throat to weaken in no time.

Tanisha didn't know what was the hardest, sucking him off or letting him enter her dripping pussy. His big dick was very pleasurable and size mattered to her.

In the middle of being sucked, Markus could feel the nut getting ready to burst. It was a rare thing, and Tanisha welcomed it. He was going to pull out directly before releasing but couldn't.

She began jerking his dick slower with both hands, and moved him inside her mouth deeper so he could shoot off in her. He moaned louder. She felt his fingers, first combing through her hair then tightening and holding her head steady. He exhaled and his stress was released with all the sticky substance he was pumping into her mouth.

One thick line of saliva mixed with semen was dangling down the side of her mouth. She wiped the moisture off her mouth with a finger and gave Markus a pathetic look. They laughed. She loved sucking him off. Markus was such a dude.

She had seen DVD's where he dominated women to the point

where when he was finished pussies looked like they needed plastic surgery. She had seen him fuck women for hours, two or three at a time. Alternating from pussy to mouth to anal, Markus would stick his dick wherever else he could. Tonight however, she dominated him. He busted off so quickly, the fastest he ever done with her. Possibly with anyone, and although she didn't get a chance to have her own orgasm, his was more pleasurable to her than her having one herself.

"You are so fucking big, Mr. Excitement," she smiled, getting off her knees.

Tanisha was a very attractive brown skinned woman. She stood at a model's five feet ten inches, most of that being legs. She was twenty-four years old, a high school dropout who watched a lot of the Discovery channel, and read National Geographic's, along with Time magazine.

She was a good listener, and Markus talked about his issues with her. She didn't live too far from him, and was a very important person in Markus's life. Tanisha stared at him with a quizzical look.

"I gotta do a couple of scenes tomorrow. I'm not sure if I'm up for the challenge..." he said.

"You busted off uncharacteristically fast. Can't they do some editing if you bust off quick like that tomorrow. It's a movie, ain't it?"

"True, but they don't do much editing in porno flicks. I'm Mr. Excitement because I got staying power. If I can't measure up, I might lose a lot of work. Smut Central Entertainment is the big leagues."

He looked at Tanisha while he was talking. Starting at her feet, Markus's eyes traveled up her long legs, finally looking her in the eyes. She smiled.

Markus was the closest thing to a true male friend. He never propositioned her for sex since he was always getting it. All he required was her company and she always welcomed Markus's huge dick. Starting with her biological father, through various step-fathers and even a couple of her uncles and cousins, Tanisha's past was filled with men who took advantage of her.

She was wearing a pair of silk boxers and a bra. She had a good looking smile that Markus loved. She was wearing it when she spoke.

"You never asked me for sex before."

"I know, sorry," he apologized. "I needed to see if I would blackout again."

"Hmm, you didn't blackout."

"True, I busted off way too quick though. I might as well have blacked out. What am I gonna do tomorrow?" He asked, sounding weak.

"Shit, Mark! You're gonna fuck. That's what you're gonna do. Stay here tonight. Get a good night's sleep. When you wake up tomorrow, I'll make you pancakes, and you can make the protein concoction stuff that you drink. Then you'll be ready. What else can you do but that?"

"True…"

Markus curled up on the couch. Tanisha wanted to tell him to sleep in the bedroom with her, but he was snoring softly. He seemed exhausted. She knew it was more of a mental thing than anything physical. She bent and kissed his bald head then went to her bedroom. Tanisha sat on the queen size bed, grabbed the television remote control, and began watching the Discovery channel.

After work that Monday, Dr. Nancy Adler had a date. She was

being courted by this lawyer, a man she met at a social function two months ago. He was white and in his mid forty's. Ernest Preston, a criminal lawyer. He had many interesting stories about criminals he represented, including a famous mafia hit-man.

The case was all over the news. Nancy didn't care much for the guy but she had not been dating much. She enjoyed the flirting and his stories. He served his purpose. Walking out of an East Village Japanese restaurant in the pleasantly cool night air, they strolled through Washington Square Park.

Nancy listened to Ernest Preston's point of view on current events, and his cases. Soon they were out of the park and walking down 6th Avenue. Nancy saw the blinking lights of an adult video shop.

"Let's go inside," she said.

Ernest shrugged. He had been trying to get inside Nancy's panties since they met. Her face wasn't much but her body was hot. That was all. Ernest was waiting for the opportunity to invite her over to his place and get in between her legs. Nancy always seemed more interested in his conversation than anything else. Now she wanted to go in a sex shop.

Ernest's mind was moving fast as he opened the door for Nancy. He followed closely behind her, and was surprised when she asked for something specific.

"I want a movie with Mr. Excitement in it. Do you know who he is?"

The woman shook her head pointing to the Black porn section. She directed her to where all the Mr. Excitement titles were. The psychiatrist picked up *Booty World volume 18* and another DVD called, *A World According to Mr. Excitement volume 1*.

"Black porn stars…? Are you getting jungle fever?"

"No, I have a client whose occupation is adult entertainment. I'm not curious. Think of it as research," Nancy laughed.

"Curious? I didn't say a thing about curious. Curious about what, his dick, black dick…?"

"Do I detect a touch of jealousy, Ernest Preston?"

"I'd say maybe a bit of it, Nancy. You have a real live porn star as a client. What's he seeing a shrink for?"

"First off, I'm a psychiatrist. Shrink is such a derogatory word. Second, I can't divulge his reason for seeing me. I never disclose information or discuss them in idle chatter."

Nancy winked at Ernest. When she turned to the cashier and handed her a credit card, she frowned. After they left the sex shop she asked Ernest to hail her a cab. When a cab pulled over, she kissed him lightly on the cheek.

"It's been very enjoyable as usual," she waved.

"Yes very," he said with outright disapproval. "I guess you will go home and cuddle to a pillow and this Mr. Excitement fellow."

"Perhaps," she said after he shut the cab door. She let the cab's window down. "Or I might cuddle to a dildo, a black one."

Ernest faked a laugh then snarled as the cab rolled away.

Nancy settled in her mid-town, high rise apartment and readied for a shower. Once her shower commenced she smiled, touching herself while she lathered and washed her body. She never fingered herself to the point where she would have an orgasm. Tonight she allowed the shower's raining to stimulate her. Thinking about all the men she found attractive, but would never have. Nancy held her pussy lips open. The spraying water hit her smooth, sensitive skin, giving her clitoris, and inner walls exposure. She was very slow when it came to getting to know a man.

While she was in the shower playing with her sexual portion, Nancy thought about her client, Markus Johnson. It was a good fantasy for her. She rubbed her clit as the water sprayed until her legs shook uncontrollably. Suddenly she stopped. It had been the longest time since she had a man inside her. She felt like she wanted that sensation instead of fingers, and the spraying water. It was one of the most refreshing showers she had ever had. She laughed at herself when she stepped out the shower. She didn't want to cum by herself, Nancy reached for a towel.

"I'm such a naughty, naughty girl. You are nasty, Nancy."

The words easily slipped from her tongue as she examined herself in front of the full length bathroom mirror.

It was close to midnight and Nancy yawned before reaching for the remote control of her DVD player. She inserted *A World According to Mr. Excitement volume one*, propped pillows up against her antique headboard, and pressed play.

Nancy watched until she felt tempted to retrieve her dildo that had been purchased two years ago. She walked over to the closet with her eyes on the video.

"You were amply named, Markus Johnson," Nancy uttered at the screen. "A world according to Mr. Excitement, indeed…"

The movie she was watching was getting her very excited. Her pussy was glistening with moisture as she reached to retrieve the once forgotten sex-toy. Nancy was aware that once she pushed it in her a little she would cum instantly.

She didn't do it. Nancy felt way too tired to get the toy from the box kept way back in her closet. It had been a very eventful day for her, she thought, walking back to the bed. She curled under the warm cover, and fell into a pleasant sleep.

Mr. Excitement atop her with his massive penis inside her, replayed on her mind as she slept. She dreamt of him looking into her dark blue eyes. Her legs were stretched open, as far as they could go. She was slowly stroking the huge thing between his legs, moving it closer toward her moist opening.

05

Markus awoke on Tanisha's couch around nine Tuesday morning. He was completely refreshed and full of vigor. Tanisha was rummaging through pots and pans in her kitchen, possibly preparing to make the pancakes she had promised.

He went to the bathroom, relieved himself then took a long shower. After the shower he wrapped a towel around his waist, heading into the kitchen with an erection. Tanisha stood by the stove, warming a griddle. The pancake batter was already whipped.

Markus crept closer to her. He knew nothing was underneath the white Victoria Secrets silk robe she was wearing. Tanisha slept completely naked. He rushed in quickly before she could turn around.

"Don't move." He pushed up her robe, exposing the thickness of her ass. "Bend over, nice and slow. I wanna see those lips split open."

She was breathing hard, but doing exactly what he told her. His hands were on her butt cheeks. Markus's tongue was flicked between them. He slid it up and down then poked inside her moistness.

"Oh yes, Markus. Keep it right there…!" Tanisha moaned.

She enjoyed penetration more than getting licked. Markus knew exactly what she was all about. He didn't stay on his knees for long. He wanted her to be thoroughly wet before he entered.

"My God…!" She gasped when he was inside her.

"I thought you were an atheist," Markus whispered. Tanisha smiled seductively.

His dick was too long and had huge girth. He entered Tanisha and she was dripping wet. Markus was the first man she had fucked with an urge to have him nut inside her because she appreciated him as a person. He wasn't a family member molesting her. He wasn't some guy with a few hundred bucks to spend in a dingy VIP room at some club.

"Your dick is… my God!" She yelled.

She held on to the stove when she felt his dick penetrating her deeply. Markus rarely entered completely because he knew that would only ignite pain. He only wanted to give Tanisha pleasure. She bent her knees when he pushed slowly inside her.

Tanisha was bent over the stove and Markus was slowly thrusting his dick halfway in her pussy then pulling out. He felt the inside of her warming then she got hot and wetter until her pussy was slippery. Suddenly her insides burst with the juices of her orgasm. A tidal wave of fluid squirted out and down his legs.

She erupted like a volcano, like her juices were being ejected out a fire hydrant. He thrust a little harder. Her head rocked back and forth as she came hard. She was a squirter. Tanisha could have been a lucrative woman making movies in the porn industry but he made sure she never did a porno flick again. Tanisha was worth more than fucking on film.

Her long legs shook as she finished her orgasmic ritual. Shaking her round ass until her body convulsed. She fell to the floor. Skeptically she moved away from the dick that made her gush.

Tanisha got on the kitchen floor, and raised her long quivering legs in the air while lying on her back.

"Come get more of this," she said.

She wanted to make him cum and knew she didn't. He was before her rock hard. The way he was before he entered earlier. She was on the kitchen floor motioning a hand toward her dripping muffin, extending the invitation.

"I gotta save myself for work… If you get my meaning…" he said, grabbing the towel.

Wrapping it around his waist, he held a hand out for Tanisha.

"What was that practice?" She asked shaking her head.

"Yes," he nodded.

"I'm a crash test dummy now, huh?" She laughed getting up on her own.

"No," he said with sincerity. "You are my friend. Look! The pan is burning!"

The kitchen was soon filled with smoke. The smoke detector went off. Markus ran to the living room to silence it. Tanisha took the griddle off the stove, ran water, and put it in the sink.

"Fuck this!" She said while the kitchen sink was running. "Let's get breakfast on the way. I'll accompany you to work."

"Are you sure?" he asked. "You know how you got the last time."

"I know, I know," she said, waving a reassuring hand at him. "I ain't even gonna trip like that no more. Shit, we're friends and I know what your job entails."

They took a shower together, lathering each other's body, and rinsing each other off. After the shower, they got dressed, and went to a local diner they frequented. The shooting was at noon. They had plenty of time.

After breakfast, they rushed to the porn shoot. The hotel suite was in a decent hotel in the Times Square area. The suites Smut Central Entertainment rented were usually spacious and the best the hotel in question had to offer. Markus and Tanisha were in the elevator heading for the penthouse suite.

"I was gonna ask if you were nervous," she began. "But then I was like, I don't want you thinking about whatever triggers those blackouts."

"Well, what you said got me thinking," Markus said, frowning. "I don't feel lightheaded. I gotta make it through the next couple of hours."

"What do you be thinking about anyway?" She asked before she answered her own question. "Yeah, you told me earlier, some girl you met a few days ago, right? What's so special about her?"

"Besides being the most beautiful thing on the planet...? I don't know..."

"Shit Mark, you fuck all forms of bitches all the time. Ain't any of them any more beautiful than the next? What am I?" Tanisha laughed.

"You're chopped liver. Isn't that how the saying goes?"

Markus winced when she bopped him on the side of his head.

"Sorry Tanisha. You are beautiful. The women I fuck on the job are the same but, this girl is different. I don't know what it is about her. She makes me think about things... my past and people and places…"

"Oh," she mumbled without really understanding what he meant.

She knew Markus went to see some shrink but they didn't speak much about it. She figured it was stupid of her to begin mentioning stuff now. He was trying to focus and not have another one of those attacks anytime soon.

"Think about me when you're fucking today. I'll be watching," Tanisha smiled.

"Think about you? Hah, fat chance! I'm doing a scene with Vonchell today. Wait 'til you see Vonchell," Markus said, waiting for another bop across the head but none was forthcoming.

The elevator door opened and they walked down a long hall to the suite. Tanisha put an ear to the door before Markus reached for the doorknob.

"I don't hear no fucking," she said in a naïve way.

"Once I punch the time clock, you'll hear a lot of it."

Markus opened the door. The staff from Smut Central Entertainment was setting their audio and video equipment. There were only a handful of people standing around, but the suite had many rooms. Markus didn't see any of the professional girls around, they must be in another room getting ready, he thought. Markus felt Tanisha grab his hand. He looked at her, said, "Thanks for coming with me."

He saw Audra, his agent with a slim cigarette in her mouth. She was discussing things with his boss, the forever shady, Tony Tee-Neck Jersey.

"There's my boy!" Tee-Neck yelled when Audra pointed to Markus. "Come over here, Excitement."

"Did that white dude with the receding hairline just called you, boy?" Tanisha said with a huge frown.

"I don't like being called boy."

He didn't like being poor either. Smut Central Entertainment was giving him more money than any adult entertainment film company he worked for. They paid him like he was white.

Markus was in an industry where white women got more money than men. Smut Central however valued the worth of a man with a huge dick and super staying power. They did little of the editing tricks the other companies did.

Most of their films had a theme. Smut Central's movies had an actual storyline, unheard of in modern day porn. They were full featured triple X films, and featured women who were ethnic and mostly exotic. These women looked more like models, angels who graced the ground mortals walked on. They weren't the average hos he fucked for small change once upon a time. This was the second gig he had with Smut Central, and didn't want to make a mess of things.

Audra gave Markus the fakest smile. Her eyes were saying, don't fucking faint on me this time. Audra took the slim cigarette out her mouth long enough to blow a long stream of smoke into Markus's face.

"Audra, the pleasure is all yours," he said, waving a hand in front of his nose before he bent and kissed her hand.

A college graduate who represented a couple of weak basketball players, and a few B movie actors, Audra was a light-skinned black woman in her thirties. She considered Markus a B movie actor. Short but not fat, Audra wasn't a bad looking woman.

Without her heavily medicated bifocals and dressed for the occasion, Audra could pass for a video hoochie. Markus wasn't sexually attracted to his agent, but would like nothing better than fuck the hell out of her one good time, just to hear her scream. Markus looked at his boss.

"Hey Tee-Neck, what's going down?"

"You are," he smiled. "On Vonchell... And this time let's hope you get back up," Tee-Neck laughed.

A spitting image of an aging mafia boss, Tee-Neck possibly was. Markus had no clue as to who Tee-Neck was. He knew Tee-Neck didn't actually direct the films. Tee-Neck owned Smut Central Entertainment, but pretended he did not.

Daisy Lace, a skinny white woman was the real director, but Tee-Neck got the credit as director, and producer. Daisy, the artist in the company, played the role of owner.

Markus paid little attention to the small talk in the room. It was clear by the way the staff was preparing the sound equipment, cameras and how the lights were place. The shooting would begin shortly.

Daisy Lace had a vision for this particular film. They were doing a few scenes with little dialogue this time for a compilation video. The norm in the porn business was to simply recycle scenes from previous films then put hours worth on a DVD.

Not Smut Central for they were innovative, and did fresh scenes all the time. There was nothing but drop-dead gorgeous, dark, and light ebony skinned women, all virgins to the camera.

Each scene started with an interview followed by the newbie getting initiated into the world of porn by Mr. Excitement's dick. Daisy Lace asked questions about their promiscuity and what they thought about Mr. Excitement fucking the hell out of them. The interviews and oral scenes had been done a couple of days beforehand. Markus had blacked out when they were about to get vaginal penetration on tape. Daisy Lace told him to prepare for the scene. They were about to take the filming where they had left off yesterday.

"Where's Vonchell?" Markus asked the director.

"I'm over here."

Markus heard the sweet voice. He turned toward the balcony door. His sight landed on slender curves and chocolate milk. Vonchell slinked away from the balcony. She trotted to him wearing only a pair of stiletto heels.

"I was admiring the skyline. This is only the second time I've been to New York," she said, her hands on hips.

"That's right. You're from Germany, right?" He asked, slowly recollecting her status.

Although she spoke perfect English, Vonchell had more than a touch of an accent. She was born and raised in Germany on a military base. Her father was a Black American soldier, and her mother native German. Vonchell was raised the proverbial army brat. Markus wondered what turned her to porn.

He didn't care to know and didn't ask Vonchell much about her past. Markus was more concerned about her nice sized heart shaped ass. Her face was breathtaking, wide hazel colored eyes, light auburn shoulder length hair, small waist, and thirty-six B's. Her sensuous five foot-six, weighing about a buck-twenty-five frame, was enough to sacrifice an arm, leg or good marriage to fuck. Doing her along with the other was on the schedule. This feat would get him a nice piece of cash.

"Don't faint on me this time, Mr. Excitement," Vonchell purred. "And don't hold back neither. Don't let my tight little pussy fool you. I like it deep, rough, hard…"

Markus couldn't wait to get inside Vonchell. All he had to do was keep his mind on the nice shape in front of him while concentrating on what was between her lick-able legs.

Markus turned around and saw Tanisha sitting on a chair behind the main camera. She was focused on the long leather couch that would host the sexual festivities. He blew her a kiss and lipped, "I'm gonna be thinking about you." Tanisha smiled. He figured she was good at reading lips.

06

Markus worked Vonchell's pussy and was about to move on to the next newcomer, a beauty, named Entice. Vonchell went beyond freaky and requested anal during the taping. Markus was more than happy to oblige. The director didn't mind and kept the cameras rolling. With the energy these two had on camera, the scene would be classic.

Tanisha winced while watching Vonchell take the huge dick in her ass with nothing but a little drip of KY jelly. Vonchell was as impressive as a pro. Markus rocked back and forth, eventually letting off on top of her marvelously shaped butt.

"Cut!" the director Daisy Lace shouted.

Jealousy washed over Tanisha. Vonchell had the perfect ass to compliment the rest of her nice body. Tanisha had eaten a pussy or two in her time, doing lesbian performances at clubs, and bachelor parties. Vonchell's act made her imagine licking pussy for no payment. Tanisha thought Vonchell was beautiful but she was a dirty little thing.

"Strictly dickly…" she uttered under breath.

"Pardon me…?" Daisy said.

"Great scene," Tanisha smiled.

"Markus, get some rest. Entice is in the next room, mentally preparing for your humongous dick," Daisy laughed from the director's chair.

"I don't need any rest. Send her in, and let's make this happen," Markus smirked.

"You're fucking amazing," the director smiled at Markus. "Get the reflection panels. Let's do this scene out on the balcony," she shouted at the camera crew.

Entice was more reserved than Vonchell. A native New Yorker, she was straight out of Queensbridge housing projects in the borough of Queens. She was good looking but not on Vonchell's level. Much like Tanisha, Entice was a stripper at first, eventually escalating into adult entertainment.

Entice took a hell of a pounding from Markus. She had never been fucked the way Markus fucked her. She told him she loved him after the shoot was over. Tanisha wasn't sure if Entice was joking or not. Entice was in love with the dick.

After the filming was wrapped for the day, Markus had a few words with his agent. Then Vonchell, Entice, Tanisha and Markus found themselves in an elevator going down to the lobby.

Vonchell suggested they all go out for a bite to eat. She wanted to experience the Big Apple in full earnest. Entice wanted to be around Markus and encouraged Vonchell's suggestion. Markus looked at Tanisha, and she indicated that she wanted to go home. All of the porn she experienced during the day made her horny. She took a good look at Vonchell's ass in the jeans hugging her to the point of strangulation. The elevator hit the ground floor.

"I'm hungry," Tanisha announced because her stomach started growling.

"Let's find a restaurant," Markus nodded.

It was a beautiful New York evening and the four of them walked until they found a nice restaurant they all decided on. It was obvious during dinner that Vonchell and Entice didn't care for each other's company. Both Markus and Tanisha found the wannabe porn stars' constant bickering quite humorous.

Markus was the least talkative during dinner. He smiled at Tanisha in the middle of dinner when he felt a foot brushing against his crotch under the table. Tanisha wanted it later and he would give it to her. But when Tanisha excused herself from the table, and went to the bathroom, Markus realized it wasn't her foot. It was Vonchell's foot still sitting on his lap.

"What are you doing tonight, Mr. Excitement?" Entice asked. "I ain't doing anything, do you want some company?"

"Do you want additional company?" Vonchell asked, giving Markus another feel with her foot.

Entice stared evilly at Vonchell, who returned the look in kind. Markus grimaced. All he wanted to do now was take Tanisha home, spend some time with her, and then go back to his place. He excused himself from the table.

Markus was about to walk to the bathroom. He had to get away from the two. He had a difficult time saying no to women and wanted to think clearly. Once she caught wind of what these two women wanted to cap the night off with, Tanisha would make up his mind for him, he was sure of that.

He didn't take more than two steps from the table when he saw her. It was the beautiful woman who had triggered the flashbacks and blackouts. He couldn't believe she was in the same restaurant. They locked eyes. She turned away with disinterest, seeming not to recognize him as the guy who offered her a drink a few weeks ago.

Again Markus was lightheaded like when he drove across the Brooklyn Bridge. He attempted to reach a safe area before he blacked out. He tried to get back to his seat. He was no more than a step away from the table but it could have been a million miles away.

He saw the same two people, a man and a woman. They were waving as he was being tugged away. A little girl was between the two people, she was crying while they waved. She was crying. Somebody was pulling him away.

"Where are you taking me?" He asked the man.

He was able to turn around and took a look at the person holding him by the wrist...

Then Markus blacked out.

Markus awoke with the worst headache possible in an emergency room of a hospital. He was lying on a gurney with a bandage wrapped around his head. His vision wavered as he attempted to look around. Tanisha was sitting on a chair next to the bed. She rose as soon as he gathered himself.

"You ok, Mark?" She asked with much concern.

"What happened?" He asked, wincing when he touched the bandage on his head.

"You blacked out, again. This time your head hit the edge of a table before you fell to the floor." Markus was about to say something but Tanisha quickly added, "I know what happened. That girl was at the restaurant."

"I know she was. What was she doing there?"

"Eating, you jerk!" Tanisha blurted in irritation. "What were we doing at the restaurant? What does anyone do in a restaurant?"

"Sorry," Markus uttered. "Let's get out of here," he said, rising out of bed.

"The doctor wants to speak to you."

"For what…? So he can recommend me see a shrink. I'm already seeing one," Markus said, sounding irritated.

"What good is that doing? You are still passing out. And what is it about this bitch that makes your brain stop functioning?"

"I don't know. Maybe you should have asked her," he snapped.

"I did," she said. "I asked her quite a few things."

"What?" He worded stunned.

"I asked her a few questions." She said…

He grabbed her by the hand before she could say more, and guided her out of the emergency room.

"But the doctor…" she protested.

"Ah fuck him," Markus snapped. "Let's go to your place. I wanna know what's going on with my head…"

"How would I know?" Tanisha asked.

"Maybe something the girl told you will answer a few things."

"Maybe I'll start talking about her, and you'll pass the fuck out again," she said and yanked her hand away from him.

They were already outside. Tanisha took Markus to where his vehicle was parked. Entice was sitting in the driver's seat. When she saw them she moved over to the passenger side. Markus sat in the backseat and Tanisha drove. Markus wasn't sure where Vonchell ran off and he wasn't sure why Entice was still hanging around.

"Are you alright?" Entice asked looking back at him from the passenger side.

"Not really," he answered.

Tanisha watched him through the rearview mirror, and she realized from his worried expression that Markus was genuinely concerned.

07

Entice traveled with them to the apartment. Tanisha didn't know why they didn't take her to the train station or wherever she was staying. Entice was genuinely concerned about Markus. Vonchell had left as soon as the paramedics showed up. Tanisha held the door opened to her apartment while Entice and Markus walked inside. She nodded approvingly when Entice sat on the living room sofa.

"Nice place." Entice small talked.

"Thanks, can I get you something to drink?" Tanisha answered cordially.

"Like a beer or vodka and chaser."

"Yeah," Tanisha said and went into the kitchen. "I'll get you something stronger than beer," Tanisha responded.

They all needed to unwind. Things were crazy with Markus passing out again. This time, on the way down, he banged his head on the edge of a table. Eight stitches atop his head was living proof.

Tanisha knew that Markus took pride in his good looks.

Markus sat on the far corner of the couch by himself. There was not much coming from him. He was tense and trusted that Tanisha knew and would fix them some strong drinks. He was thinking about Tanisha when Entice moved closer to him. She placed her hand on his leg and started rubbing him. Her attempt to assuage the pain in his head did nothing to ease his mind. He glanced at her. Entice was a good looking girl. Markus wasn't about to tell her stop.

"Who was that girl?" Entice asked.

"Huh?" Markus mumbled while lost in his thoughts. "What girl?"

"The girl who made you faint. Tanisha told me there's some girl making you faint."

He laughed, "I don't know who she is."

"She didn't know you either? She said she never seen you before in her life."

"That's not true. I met her at an after hours spot, in Times Square actually."

He had spoken to this woman, offered her a drink then he had blacked out. She should have remembered. Why didn't she?

Markus mind was in overdrive when Tanisha returned having slipped into a comfortable pair of sweatpants, and sports bra. Even without sneakers, she looked like she was about to go jog or carry herself to the gym.

"She doesn't remember you. One of her friends at the table remembered you and said you were good looking," Tanisha said.

"Oh...?" Markus said grimacing.

"What's wrong, Markus?" Tanisha asked.

"My head is throbbing. Before I blacked out in the restaurant I had another flashback. This time more, um, distinctive. If you get my meaning…?"

"What are you talking about?" Entice asked, sounding confused.

Markus and Tanisha continued their conversation as if Entice wasn't there. Entice decided to stay silent and listened.

"More distinctive, what do you mean by that?" Tanisha asked with unbridled curiosity.

"You sound like my shrink," Markus smirked. "My head's on fire. I mean like it was clearer and I got more of it. There is another person in my mind."

"You mean besides your parents and that little girl?" Tanisha asked.

"Yes, but who knows if any of these people are a relation of mine or not… If you get my meaning…"

"Come on Markus, who else would you be thinking about? You can barely remember anything about yourself. You didn't even have a birth certificate until my friend forged one for you."

Tanisha was standing next to him but she eventually got on the living room carpet and began stretching.

"You got work tonight?" Markus asked.

His head was burning up. Now he wished he had talked to the doctor. Maybe he could have had some painkillers. He had to see the shrink at once. Monday seemed far away. It was still Tuesday and a few minutes past eleven at night.

Markus had no porno gigs pending. He was free till he got the call and had nothing pressing to do. The lack of excitement would drive him crazy. He was after all named, Mr. Excitement.

"I gotta work tonight. And on that note," Tanisha said, looking over at Entice while she stretched. "Want me to drop you somewhere?"

"Wait," Markus spoke before Entice could answer. "What about this girl? What is her name? You haven't told me anything?"

"I know, it can wait," Tanisha gave him a wicked grin. "I don't want you passing out any time soon." He was about to reply but she pointed a finger at him. She rose out of her split. "Don't say a fucking word. I'm the closest thing you got to family, other than your daughter. I got mystery woman's name and cell phone number. We can deal with all of this later. I don't want you passing out again. Get some rest. Stay here tonight." He reluctantly agreed with Tanisha's logic. "Come on girl, I'm gonna drop you off somewhere." Tanisha said to Entice.

"I wanna stay here with Mr. Excitement," Entice's smile, showing them all her beautiful set of teeth.

"No, we all had enough excitement for one night," Tanisha said with a cynical smile.

Entice waved goodbye to Markus with her bottom lip low. Tanisha offered to drive Entice to the closest train station. Entice declined the offer and hailed a cab once they got downstairs.

"I'm gonna keep in touch with you guys," Entice told Tanisha with a genuine smile. "I like you people."

Tanisha shrugged her shoulders. Once the cab drove off Tanisha hopped inside her car and went to work. She stripped at a place called Jingling Babes in Long Island. It wasn't an upscale club, but it wasn't a cesspool either. Markus knew the owner and he hooked her up with a job. He didn't like the shit holes Tanisha used to shake her booty in before they met.

The owner of Jingling Babes was stern and decent. There was no extracurricular activities going down in the VIP rooms, and on a good night Tanisha made as much as a thousand dollars. There were few black girls dancing at Jingling Babes, she was a commodity.

Markus watched television while Tanisha was at work. He found a bottle of codine pills in the bathroom cabinet. Tanisha used to have severe headaches and acquired the pills from a friend who was in a car accident. Markus swallowed two pills and it did the trick. The pills had him sedated and he fell into a pleasant, medicated sleep on Tanisha's bed. That was where she found him when she got home in the wee hours of the morning.

Figuring he needed some sleep, Tanisha didn't wake him. She hated her job but worked hard, earning about five hundred dollars, very good for a Tuesday night at Jingling Babes. Tuesday wasn't a money night. Some police sergeant was having a retirement party at the club. The place was packed with police officers. They weren't above dishing out dough for a pretty Black chick with long legs, and a fat ass.

Tanisha took a much needed, very long shower. After she got in bed and snuggled against Markus's back. He was half sleep but moved into her body in response.

"Get out of your clothes," she whispered.

He did so half asleep while muttering inaudibly, his voice low. It didn't matter. He was soon naked and under the covers with Tanisha.

08

Nancy Adler was at her desk typing on her laptop in her office. Markus Johnson and his dilemma stayed on her mind. Since seeing him, she had thought about him a lot. She began doing research on amnesia to refresh her memory. Nancy had not seen a patient with a case of amnesia since she began her practice ten years ago.

She figured Markus's affliction may have been caused by head trauma, maybe an event in his past, so shocking his mind blocked it out. His mind might be mending itself, and that could be the reason Markus was beginning to remember things. Nancy thoughts were spurred while typing notes. She only had one session with him and still wasn't sure what was exactly causing his conditions.

"From what I gathered during the first meeting with the client, a woman he met triggered the first flashback. A chain reaction has been set up where the flashback has triggered his blackout. Markus Johnson came into my office because of the blackouts, but he has amnesia. I think the amnesia is the catalyst. I'm quite certain hypnosis could lead us in the correct direction but the client doesn't want to involve any hypnotism." Nancy Adler typed and perused the text. The psychiatrist realized she failed to mention the unusual life Markus lived in her case notes. Also there was no telling how his past had affected the case. Finally she stopped typing and sat thinking the entire episode over, she decided she would have to purchase a few more DVD's of Mr. Excitement.

Watching them gave her the urge to touch herself. Markus's movies showed him having sex with women in every which way possible. Although she found him to be an interesting man, Nancy Adler thought his daughter's mother, Gwyneth, even more fascinating.

Nancy wanted to probe Gwyneth for additional information about Markus. She wanted to know why a woman as allegedly conservative as Gwyneth, would harbor a homeless black youth and eventually have a child with him. Gwyneth was married to a very successful businessman who had sexual issues. He was gravely ill. She didn't figure Markus Johnson or their daughter, Emily, in Gwyneth's husband's sexual situation. It all was starting to make sense.

Gwyneth's husband's sexual issues went further than having difficulties getting an erection. It had something to do with his fertility as well. Markus obviously donated sperm, she surmised. She wondered why this never came up in their sessions. Gwyneth and Markus had a child for Gwyneth and her husband.

Nancy was sure her husband's fertility had to be an issue. This was more than Gwyneth having a one night stand with some black man and deciding to keep the child. As far as Nancy could determine Gwyneth was not disclosing all there was to be told. Whether or not she would speak on the skeletons in her closet remained to be seen. The intercom on the desk beeped.

"What is it, Stephanie?" Nancy asked her secretary.

"Gwyneth Manners is here to see you."

"Of course, it's Thursday and it's six pm. Send her in, please."

Nancy rose from her desk as Gwyneth Manners opened the door and walked in.

"Welcome Gwyneth, please sit down," Nancy greeted.

Gwyneth let her fashionable, ankle length parker fall. She was wearing a tight black leather mini skirt and a leather halter top underneath. It was a revealing two piece. Nancy wasn't shocked by the attire. She only considered Gwyneth conservative in the political sense. Her lifestyle had turned more liberal with each visit.

She sat on the leather couch and dramatically crossed her legs slowly, showing Nancy that she was wearing nothing underneath the skirt. Gwyneth laughed when she saw Dr. Adler's expression.

"Do you mind if I smoke?" she asked, holding a gold cigarette holder and took a long slender cig from it.

Nancy quickly rose from the chair and went over to her desk. She grabbed a glass, the first thing she saw that would do as an ashtray and walked over to Gwyneth. She handed it to her. Nancy sat back down. She wasn't amused, watching as Gwyneth seductively placed the cigarette on the edge of her mouth. She lit it.

"How are you?" Gwyneth asked, inhaling the smoke.

"I should be asking you that," Dr. Adler said sternly.

"I'm great. Oh no, I'm not. My husband's back in the hospital," Gwyneth said without any hint of sadness.

"I'm sorry to hear about your husband. Is he going to be alright?"

"Let's hope not. How long am I supposed to endure taking care of him? He's practically a vegetable. I'm running the company singlehandedly, and doing a horrible job of it. Every stockholder and chairman is waiting for him to die so they can take what's rightfully mine right from under my nose."

"I see," Dr. Adler's responded.

"I stopped taking the lithium you prescribed. Don't look at me like that Nancy. I told you to write me a prescription for valium. And since you didn't, I found other ways of obtaining it," she said, pulling on the cigarette so hard it was all gone in no time.

She retrieved another, and lit it while Nancy eyed her with curiosity.

"I refuse to prescribe you a drug that isn't necessary for you. Lithium is all you need for your mild manic depressive illness," she frowned. "I suggest you continue to take the lithium and cease using valium. Valium is quite addictive."

"And so is lithium. Valium makes me feel better," Gwyneth snarled in frustration. "I'm dealing with so many things. Please don't start chastising me. You're the only person that I can talk to. You are my only friend in this cold world," she chuckled. Nancy quickly stifled the urge to join in the mirth.

"Now, I suggest you discuss your unauthorized drug use with your primary doctor," Nancy suggested.

"Who do you think is providing me with the valium? Don't look so shocked Nancy. I'm quite sure you do something not authorized, like smoke reefer."

"Who's the psychiatrist, and who's the patient Mrs. Manners? Our contract is a month away from expiring. Before our union comes to an end, I would like to see you more cohesive and stable. You're fidgeting. Have you had a manic episode lately?"

"I have," Gwyneth said, rising from off the couch.

She didn't realize she was fidgeting until Nancy informed her.

Gwyneth wanted to tell the psychiatrist that the lithium kept her less excitable, but also stunted her sexual appetite, and the valium made her pussy moist.

"I had one this morning," she answered, thinking.

"How severe was it?" The doctor asked.

"Severe enough to scare the household help, I broke a very expensive vase I purchased from Tiffany's. And I completely ruined the living room in a fit of rage," Gwyneth said, sounding as if she was proud of her actions. "I feel much better now. I was so stressed over my husband."

"I bet," Nancy stated mildly. "How's your daughter?"

"Simply wonderful, her father came over this morning, and picked her up. She should be back with the nanny by now."

"Did you have the manic attack before or after Markus came over?" the psychiatrist asked.

"After," Gwyneth said, bending down and grabbing her jacket. The skirt was so small Nancy saw everything. Gwyneth turned around and gave Nancy a wicked smile. "Isn't my daughter's daddy a fuckable looking thing, so beautiful, young, black and strong? Did I mention that his dick is really big?"

"No, I'm afraid you didn't. Please Mrs. Manners cease taking the valium, and continue to take the drug I prescribed for you."

"I'll consider it," Gwyneth answered.

Gwyneth was almost at the door when Nancy said, "One more thing before you go. Markus Johnson is so young, I believe he's twenty and your daughter is six going on seven."

"And...?" Gwyneth said.

"And that would mean you were sleeping with a thirteen or fourteen year old boy."

"I guess you're right. I never bothered to calculate things. I

Nancy had one other patient after Gwyneth Manners left. That session was over at eight. Nancy dismissed her secretary and turned off the lights. In the elevator going down to the lobby, she thought about Gwyneth Manners. There was one other person riding to the lobby with her. Her office was located in a skyscraper in midtown Manhattan and most of the other businesses in the building were closed hours ago.

She stepped out the elevator and into the lobby. She was about to ask the doorman to hail her a cab when her cell phone rang. The psychiatrist looked at the caller ID and didn't recognize the number.

"Hello," she said with uncertainty.

"Dr. Adler, did I call you at the wrong time?"

At first she didn't recognize the voice then she blushed. Mr. Excitement didn't speak much in his movies. It was just a lot of moaning and groaning.

"It's Markus…"

"Markus, please, call me Nancy," she sighed. "You didn't catch me at the wrong time. I'm just leaving the office. How did you get my cell phone number?"

"It's on your business card. I called your office. No one answered." Markus took a deep breath. "Listen I'll see you next Monday…"

"No," Nancy said. Her voice lightened as she continued. "What's wrong? Are you okay?"

"I'm not. I must have blacked out five or six times since I last saw you. I even blacked out in the car on my way home that same day."

"My God…!" She exclaimed.

"I know why I'm blacking out. It's this woman. I keep thinking about her and seeing her. Because of her, I'm blacking out."

"What about the flashbacks?" She queried.

"They are more distinctive, clearer. There is another person in the picture. I think I was kidnapped when I was younger," Markus said.

He had been thinking about things for quite some time. So many things were going down and transpired since the first session and he couldn't wait. He had to speak to Nancy Adler.

"I blacked out in front of Emily."

"Your daughter…?" the psychiatrist asked softly. "Is she okay? Are you okay?"

"Yes and no. Damn! I don't really know. It scared Emily but I think she's okay. I told her daddy was sick. She thinks Mr. Manners is her daddy also. So when she said, I know daddy's sick, I didn't know who she meant. My life is so fucking screwed up."

"Where are you?" Nancy asked.

Nancy was completely intrigued by Markus Johnson. He sparked her interest a thousand fold.

"I'm at a bar about to get drunk, and do something stupid."

Markus sound so defeated that Nancy was sure his affliction was getting the best of him.

"Where is the bar?"

"Brooklyn, it's in the ghetto," he laughed.

"Does the ghetto have an address?" She asked sarcastically.

"It does, but I'm not home though you can meet me where I am. You did ask because you want to meet me, right?"

"You sound self-destructive, and I want to know more. I want to help you. Your situation is more peculiar than you think."

"Okay," Markus said, giving her the address.

"Besides, I do nothing at night, but watch sitcom reruns. I'm sure your company will be more interesting than that," Nancy said, sounding sincere.

When she arrived at the address Markus had given, Nancy was very tempted to hop back inside the cab and go directly home. It was truly ghetto. She rarely frequented Brooklyn, and when she did it wasn't where Markus wanted her to meet him.

She paid the cab driver, and the cab sped off. Nancy was left standing on a street corner in very grimy area. Across from her was a housing project. Young, black males stared at her and she held on tighter to her Louie Vuitton purse. Markus was with a group of black males. It was dark but she recognized him. He spotted her. Leaving the group behind, he walked toward her. Nancy smiled. He smiled back.

"You are such a brave little vixen."

Members of his clique all knew what Markus did for a living and they would assume she was a porno bitch. Nancy was dressed conservatively, wearing a trendy red trench coat; it was open, exposing her black skirt suit and white shirt. Markus could tell she was uncomfortable.

"This isn't the sort of place for a woman like you," he smiled.

"What sort of woman am I, Markus, a white one?" She sassed.

"Yeah," he said. "I think you are white." They both grinned. "I was figuring this ain't your type of environment."

"It might not be but I'm here," she said. "You're here so I'm safe, right?"

"Shit, you were safe even if I wasn't here," Markus smiled but he was unsure of his own words.

Markus lived in a tough neighborhood. He looked behind him and saw the guys on the corner grilling them. He knew they were scheming on the white dame in their neck of the hood. Markus decided to scramble before they felt curious enough to approach them.

"My car is around the corner," he said, taking her arm and guiding her toward his vehicle.

"Where are we going?" She asked once he opened the door for her and rushed to the driver's side. Markus had a nice Lexus. She wondered why he lived in this particular neighborhood.

"Do you like Japanese?" He asked before turning on the engine.

"I like the food but not the men," Nancy laughed.

"Why not the men," he said, looking at her with a wicked grin.

"Is it because of how small their dicks are?"

"We all know how big you are Markus. Gwyneth told me. No…?" She chuckled. "I used to date a Japanese guy when I was in college. The relationship didn't go well. He wanted me to dress up like a geisha and it wasn't Halloween. That was way too kinky for me."

Markus laughed but inside he felt little humor. The relationship he had with Gwyneth wasn't anything he found humorous. Gwyneth was the sort of person who would describe how big his dick was in great detail.

Nancy didn't know how hurt he was from what she said. He shrugged his shoulders and began driving. She would never even think something like that would affect a man who fucked women on camera for a living.

Nancy knew something she said disturbed him. His mood had changed and he was silent and seemed distant for a great deal of their trip. Markus turned on the radio. They were listening to a classic rock radio station, and Nancy was shocked to hear Markus singing along with Queen.

"You have good taste in music," she said, singing along with him.

"You have good taste in the company you choose," Markus said before he switched the radio station. Rap music was thumping.

Markus was shocked when he heard Nancy utter, "You're a window shopper…" She sang along with the song and she knew the lyrics. Dr. Nancy Adler was a fan of Fifty Cent. Markus didn't see that coming.

10

They went to a quaint Japanese place in Brooklyn Heights. Markus watched Nancy who was studying him. The waitress was standing before them, waiting to take their order. Markus ordered the chicken teriyaki, and Nancy had an assortment of sushi. They agreed on the wine. The waitress came with an already uncorked and chilled bottle of rose and two wine glasses. Markus poured the Vino.

Nancy was still trying to figure out why she decided to meet Markus. He was obviously going through all forms of stuff. She decided to break the ice.

"Gwyneth is a very interesting person. You were introduced to her at a very young age."

Markus knew Nancy was expecting him to tell her something, something he didn't want to discuss. She was his shrink. He told her things he only told Tanisha.

"Gwyneth used to pick up male prostitutes, take them home,

and fuck them in front of her husband. He got his jollies watching young men fuck his wife."

"Oh my," she uttered.

"Yeah, he's old and impotent. She took me off the streets. I had already been out on the street for about six months or so. I was hungry and dirty, with not a lot of options. She took me to her three story penthouse apartment, the one overlooking Central Park, cleaned and fed me. I wasn't sure at first, Gwyneth wasn't a bad looking woman and they clothed me, sheltered me and gave me money. I stayed that night and never left till I was eighteen."

"Oh," Nancy said, looking shocked. "So, you would have sexual relations with Gwyneth in front of Mr. Manners. That sounds really sick."

"I was young. I had nothing. I never knew much about anything…if you get my meaning. Shit, I don't even remember how I ended up in the orphanage. Sleeping with Gwyneth was better than being on the streets, and sleeping on park benches. Mr. Manners hired a tutor to educate me," Markus said, giving Nancy a wide grin. "I can see it in your eyes. You're wondering why I speak as well as I do."

"How do you get along in life without an identity? Do you have a driver's license or any other form of ID?"

"Yes, a friend of mine, Tanisha, knows a person who can get a fake license, birth certificate, or whatever you want. While I was with Gwyneth and her husband I was more like a sex slave, a prisoner. I didn't get out much."

"Sickening," Nancy said in disgust.

"If it wasn't for them, I don't know where I would be now."

Apprehension set in and Markus seemed like he didn't want to continue. Nancy reached over the table and touched his hand lightly. He looked at her soft eyes and continued speaking.

"She used to give me to some of her friends. These women would take me for a day, a night, and I would do things with them, sexual shit. Fuck them, eat their pussies. They paid me. They were all older women, some of them were good looking but most of them were horrible looking."

"You've lived a rather bizarre life."

She didn't know what else to say. The conversation they were having was disturbing. She was already on her second glass of wine. Markus wasn't drinking anything.

"Your daughter, Emily…"

"I don't wanna talk about Emily. She's the only good thing I have. She's the best part of me," he said, cutting her inquiry short.

"Okay," she said feebly. "I understand."

"I wanna talk about my flashbacks, and about this woman. This woman I keep thinking about."

"The woman who initially triggered the reemerging memories or flashbacks, you encountered her again. Where did you see her?"

"I saw here first in a restaurant in Times Square. I had just come from filming a scene. She was sitting at a table with some other people. I took one look at her and began seeing things, those two people…"

"Your parents," she interjected.

"Possibly, I saw the little girl also. It seemed like the same thing every time. The flashback continued. I was being yanked away from them, like I told you before, but this time I got a look at the person who was taking me away."

"What did this person look like?" She probed.

"He was a white man, an old man. He had a beard. I remember that, and he had a mean looking face. I was scared of him. I didn't wanna go wherever he was dragging me. The people were waving goodbye. At first I thought I was being kidnapped. Now I'm not so sure. If those people I saw were my parents, why would they be waving while I was being kidnapped?"

"I'm not sure, Markus. I know this hypnotist who could…"

"No hypnosis," he said with a touch of anger. "No hypnosis. Haven't we gone over this before?"

"Just once," she said with a stern voice. She softened up immediately. "I'm only trying to help. Why do you think I'm here?"

"Because you like Japanese food," he smirked. "Because Gwyneth said my dick is big," he said and Nancy blushed then frowned. "Sorry," he said with sincerity.

"Gwyneth didn't have to tell me about your anatomy. I purchased a couple of your movies."

"Oh did you…? What do you think about them?"

"What is there to think? I watched the movies. I've seen pornography before. What made you get into this line of work?"

"I guess Gwyneth is responsible. One of her friend's had connections in the porn biz. After doing things with these women, I'd talk with them. Nancy, you know what?"

"What Markus?"

"Sex always seemed second nature to me. It's like I've done it before. And I'm not talking about fucking. I mean like I've been in front of the camera before. When I went to Brazil to do a film, I could have sworn I'd been there before. Like when I was younger, much younger."

"That's interesting, Markus. Maybe you have. So much of your life is a big void. What you mentioned about sex being second nature to you is intriguing." She paused.

The waitress came with the food. When the waitress left, she continued. "I know this hypnotist…" Markus grimaced. She laughed.

They ate and talked. Nancy guided the conversation while they ate, chatting to him about herself for a while.

"This woman, the one that triggers the flashbacks and the black outs, describe her to me."

"She is complete and utter perfection." Markus felt lightheaded thinking about her. "Funny as it may seem, I haven't gotten a good look at her…"

"Because you are always in La-La-Land directly after an encounter," Nancy said, smiling.

Markus laughed. "I have her phone number. I haven't used it yet. Should I?" He asked the shrink.

"Of course you should, but only when you are ready. What do you think she will have to say?"

"I don't know." He was silent for a moment. "Do you think I blacked out from some longing for her? I never felt for a person the way I feel for her."

"Markus, my love," she said in a playful manner. "You don't even know this woman. How could you possibly feel anything? Maybe you do know her."

"That's what I'm thinking. But my friend, Tanisha, assured me Michelle said she never saw me before."

"Michelle, is that her name? I would like to meet this woman who you find so alluring. You've been with hundreds. What is physical sex when compared to the emotions and mentality involved in loving someone?"

Nancy thought about what she said then giggled. She was beginning to sound like a silly schoolgirl on a first date. She had drunk the whole bottle of wine. Markus had not taken a sip from his glass. "Are you trying to get me drunk?" She laughed.

"I don't have to try. It seems like you're getting drunk all by yourself."

"Let me drive you home," Markus offered when they walked out the restaurant.

"Tempting," she said, giving him her best rendition of a seductive look. "I'll catch a cab. We must keep this relationship professional."

"Of course," he said.

It was late and there were few cars moving through the streets. A yellow cab pulled up after he whistled it down. He opened the door. She slipped into the cab. Markus kissed her on the lips before shutting the door. She was caught completely off guard, but that didn't stop her from closing her eyes, and allowing herself to get lost within the act of the kiss.

"Remember sex is my profession, Dr. Adler. So indulging me will be keeping it professional in any event," he smiled and the cab drove off.

Markus was singing along with the radio while driving back home. He had a very nice time with Nancy. She was a good listener, but she was a psychiatrist. Her job was to listen. Markus wasn't on the time clock while they were talking. He figured they had gone out on a date, it wasn't a session. Or was it? He wasn't sure. He was physically attracted to her. He decided to tie the euphoria he was feeling to that, and nothing more. He parked the Lexus and strolled to his residence.

It was close to one in the morning. The local drug dealers were not out hustling. Markus's hood was deserted. He lived in a small three story building with a liquor store located on the first floor. He hadn't actually touched his wine during dinner and wanted some. Unfortunately, the liquor store was closed and he did not have anything strong upstairs. Markus let himself inside the apartment and his cell phone rang. He looked at the caller ID then answered.

"Agent extraordinaire, what can I do for you?"

"Flattery will get you nowhere with me Markus Johnson," Audra snapped.

"Why are you calling me at this ungodly hour, if not for flattery?" He asked flatly.

"I got another gig for you. Smut Central Entertainment wants you in their office first thing Monday morning," she said, hanging the phone up.

What a bitch, he thought. She had brought him good news. Smut Central wanted him for another gig. He was quite certain he had already been paid for the last movie. Smut Central paid on time and paid exceptionally well. He needed all the money he could make.

Markus took off his jacket and shirt. He stomped a bold roach crawling on the floor.

"I gotta get out of this roach infested dump!" He yelled at the flattened pest.

The place wasn't entirely a dump, but the neighborhood left much to be desired. He wanted to live in a different location. The freaky time he spent with Gwyneth and Mr. Manners left him with higher aspirations.

Before he went to sleep he had an overwhelming urge to call the former mystery woman, Michelle. It was way too late and he gave up on the idea realizing he was a complete stranger to her. His thoughts made him feel woozy. Flopping on his bed in jeans and boots, Markus tried thinking of other things. He closed his eyes trying to shut out the woman who kept sending him back to a past he had somehow forgotten.

Markus dreamt that he was a child no older than nine, in a room full of hundreds of other children. The room was stuffy and cluttered. He could barely move. It was dark and the children were crying. He could hardly hear himself thinking. He felt he should be crying as well but there were no tears.

There were no windows in the room, but a dim light shone from an opening. It was a doorway and the door wasn't locked. He was elbow to elbow with so many other children he couldn't reach the door if he tried. It was the only way out.

The air was nauseatingly infested with the scent of rotten food, stale urine and feces. Winged insects, possibly flies, were numerous and everywhere, almost apart of the air itself. If you opened your mouth you would take the insects in with the air. They would go all the way down and into your stomach. Markus was sure of it.

He harbored an overwhelming urge to bite and scratch his way through the bodies but didn't have the strength. He felt claustrophobic, began panting, everything was moving in and getting closer. He was heaving in gulps of air. All the kids were sucking all the oxygen. The only ventilation was the half-inch crack at the bottom of the door.

Markus had seen the door once when he was first forced into the room. He felt a rush of the freshest air coming from it directly before it closed. By then he was practically in the middle of the room, surrounded by hundreds of children. He had to get to the door, but couldn't move an inch.

He opened his mouth a bit too much and thousands of winged insects went down inside him. He screamed. Flies, they were flies. Hundreds of thousands of flies, all the flies in the room flew into his mouth and down into his stomach.

Markus heard some of the flies saying things. Most of them

were buzzing, speaking unrecognizable phrases, but some he heard clearly.

They were saying, "This way, he has opened his mouth, now we can escape." All Markus wanted to do was reach the door. Markus woke drenched in sweat. He looked around the room, looked for the children, looked for the door, the crack under the door, the light.

"Shit," he said, wiping some sweat from his forehead. "It was only a weird-ass dream."

After some thinking, Markus realized that he never remembered a dream as detailed as he remembered this one. He never even thought about his dreams after he awoke.

"Strange," he whispered. "Very fucking strange..." He looked at his alarm clock. "Stranger still, I only slept for a half hour." He rose and walked over to the window, opened the blinds. "No," he thought aloud. The light of day made his eyes squint. "It's the very next day." He looked at his watch. "Shit!" he exclaimed. "It's fucking Saturday afternoon."

Markus wasn't ready to except the reality of things. He went to sleep at around one Friday morning. It was Saturday afternoon, just a few minutes past one-thirty. "What the fuck is wrong with me?" He asked himself.

Lucky for him, there was nothing pending until Monday morning. He had to go to Manhattan to the Smut Central Entertainment office bright and early and he had to see his shrink at six that evening. This whole thing was bizarre. He had never slept that length of a time in his life. Markus called Tanisha.

"Hello," she greeted. Once she realized it was Markus she barked. "I was calling you all fucking day yesterday. Why didn't you answer your phone?"

"I just got up," he said, yawning.

"Fuck today, I'm talking about yesterday."

"Stop yelling. I'm serious. I was asleep for over twenty-four hours."

"That's fucking incredible," she blurted. "Damn," Tanisha said, calming down. "You serious…?"

"Yes. What's wrong with you, yelling at me like you're my wife or some shit? Where are you?"

"Don't ask me where I am, like I'm your wife or some shit. I'm getting my nails did. Afterwards I'm going shopping. Why don't you join me?" She said in a pleasant tone.

"Maybe," he uttered with uncertainty. Tanisha had a strange tone to her voice. She sounded way too nice. "You never asked me to go shopping with you before. What's the special occasion?" He asked sounding suspicious.

"The special occasion is I ran out of money," she said, laughing at her own joke. "Seriously Mark, I was worried about you. I haven't heard from you all day yesterday. Come meet me at the nail shop, you know where I get my nails done."

"It's gonna take me an hour at least…"

"Fine," she interrupted. "I'll get a pedicure and a massage also, to pass the time. I'll be here. Hurry..."

"Right," Markus tossed his cell phone on the bed.

He needed to take a very long shower and he needed to clear his head. The dream was very disturbing, and the fact that he had slept for over twenty-four hours was very out of the ordinary.

Markus took a very long shower. He realized he was outright starving once he got dressed and was putting on his jewelry. He needed a shave. Moving his hand over his head, Markus could feel the early stages of follicles. He glanced at his watch, remembering how impatient Tanisha was. He didn't want to keep her waiting. The sooner they met, the sooner he could get something to eat.

Feeling hungry, Markus jogged down the stairs, and walked out the front door of the building. It was sunny. He left a pair of shades in the car. He was going to put them on. He wore a light spring jacket but didn't need it. It was a beautiful day. He felt like jogging to his car, but strolled up the block instead. Some dude was sitting on the hood of the Lexus. He wanted to yell at dude, but recognized the guy by what he was wearing, and kept his cool. It was Sparks, a friend.

Sparks usually wore a white tee shirt, a fitted hat of some sort; rocking colors that would match whatever Nike sneakers he decided to wear. Today he had on gray and white fitted from a Negro league team and gray, blue and orange Air Max.

Sparks saw how Markus focused on his sneaks and said, "I'm wearing these for the first time and the last. You'll never see me wear these shits again this year. Nike is running out of things for me to purchase. I might have to switch brands or walk around barefooted."

Before Markus could say, get off the hood of my car, Sparks raised one of his hands dramatically, and pointed a finger down. Markus followed the finger until he saw where it ended.

"What the fuck…!" Markus said walking around his car, looking at the tires. All of his tires were flat, someone had slashed his tires!

"They got you good, nigga."

"Who got me?" Markus questioned with anger.

"Probably the nigga's you were hanging out with the other night, that's who," Sparks laughed. "Hate is all around us young Jedi. Jealousy, envy, shit nigga, the way you floss round here with all the platinum and diamonds… This Lexus and all your talk about the bitches you fuck in the movies…"

"Sparks, I don't brag," Markus said softly.

"You don't have to brag. Just walking around this hood where niggas be seeing and knowing, is enough. You need to keep a lower profile, my man," Sparks said, fumbling in his pocket. "Get a Dutch Master or something," he continued, producing a nice, meaty bag of green marijuana.

Sparks began dangling the bag in Markus's face like a carrot. He was the neighborhood drug dealer and Markus was the horse. Markus didn't feel like smoking weed. The tires on his Lexus had been slashed, and he wanted to know who did it. In the past, he never had any sort of situation or problems in his hood. He mentally vowed to have problems with whoever slashed his tires.

He walked across the street, went inside the corner store, and bought a cigar. Markus was a casual user and gave the cigar to Sparks. Unraveling the Dutch, Sparks was soon rolling. Then he lit the nice sized blunt.

"It was probably that nigga, Cali. He's always talking cross about you," Sparks said between pulls. He passed the blunt to Markus.

"Cali," Markus uttered the name, inhaled weed and continued. "I don't have any problems with Cali."

"He gotta problem with you. Didn't he used to fuck with that stripper bitch? What's the bitch's name, Tanisha?" Sparks asked.

"No way," Markus said, passing the blunt, and pausing for a beat. "Damn… Well I think he did something in the VIP room with her when she was going down that route. If you get my meaning…?"

"Going down that route…? Nigga, you fuck bitches on film for money, and you say shit like going down that route? When a bitch is turning tricks…?" Sparks let out a loud laugh with the smoke. He laughed so hard he almost dropped the blunt during the exchange.

"True," he mumbled. "She doesn't do that type of stuff anymore."

"Not that you know of," he said, correcting Markus. "Fuck her. This ain't about how many dicks she sucks at the club. A nigga like Cali can hold a grudge against you for some petty shit like this though. We all know you be over her crib slaying that on the regular. Maybe he tried to get another blowjob and she told him to be easy. That's all it takes."

"This shit is dumb," Markus blurted.

"Dumb or not, look at your tires. Aren't those Pirellis?" He questioned, looking at Markus's deflated tires. "Here," he said, passing the blunt.

"Yep," Markus confirmed. "Slashing tires is some real bitch shit. Only women do shit like that."

"Needless to say, I think it was him. Weren't you hanging with Cali the other night?" Sparks asked, snatching the blunt from Markus.

"Hmm, hmm, I was," Markus slowly nodded.

"There you go. You probably mentioned Tanisha, right?"

"Shit! I gotta meet Tanisha now. Damn! I gotta get these flats fixed."

Markus watched as Sparks broke out in another hearty fit of laughter. Sparks sucked on the roach before speaking.

"Nigga, you need new tires. You can't patch those. Where you gotta go, my car is around the block?"

Markus thanked Sparks for the ride but he knew his friend wanted to tag along for more than doing him a favor. He was sure Sparks would make moves on Tanisha. In the hood, friends weren't below trying to get some pussy anyway they could. Tanisha wasn't a whore, at least not anymore. But who knows what Sparks thought in that criminal brain of his. Markus took another look at his tires. He needed a ride. Sparks was the closest thing to a ride at the present moment.

Markus gave Sparks the directions to the nail shop. It was in the East Village in Manhattan, a place Sparks rarely ventured. Sparks called himself a businessman. He was well respected in the hood. Markus smoked weed. If it weren't for local drug dealers like Sparks, he wondered how he would acquire the illegal narcotic.

Markus was very high. He wasn't sure what sort of weed they smoked, but that shit was potent. They finished off another blunt in the car. Once they reached Manhattan, Sparks was looking for a store to purchase another cigar.

"Why don't you buy a box of cigars?" Markus asked.

"Man, I like my cigars fresh."

Sparks was a very interesting dude, Markus decided as they walked into the nail parlor. He saw Tanisha sitting in the waiting area with her head inside a Cosmopolitan magazine. Markus hailed her. She acknowledged him with a smile. When she saw who was with him she frowned at Sparks.

"What the fuck is he doing with you?" She asked as they walked out the nail parlor.

Sparks was a few steps ahead of them. He was dumping the contents of a Dutch Master cigar, leaving a trail for them to follow like bread crumbs.

"I needed a ride. Cali slashed my tires," Markus told her.

"Cali…?" she gasped.

"Yeah Cali," he said, eyeing Tanisha with suspicion.

She was never short on words, but this time she had nothing to say. Markus wasn't sure why and he decided to change the subject.

"You said you wanted to go shopping. Where…? In the East Village…?"

"Yeah," she answered. "You said you slept for over twenty-four hours. How crazy is that?"

"I don't know how crazy. I guess I better discuss this with my shrink on Monday."

"Did you call Michelle yet?" She asked changing the conversation's direction.

"Nope," he said with simplicity.

"You scared?" She asked.

Markus didn't answer. Sparks was about to light the blunt but Tanisha said, "Jerk, you gonna get arrested! This is not the hood. You can't just smoke drugs out in the open."

"I'll take my chances," Sparks said, smiling at her.

"No you won't," Tanisha said sternly.

She held her hand out, and Sparks reluctantly handed her the blunt.

"This is appalling," Sparks barked as Tanisha and Markus broke out in raucous laughter.

13

After a couple of hours of walking around, Markus knew Tanisha didn't truly want to go shopping. First, they walked two blocks from the nail parlor and got something to eat at BBQ's. Markus was starving; he ravaged his meal in silence while Sparks and Tanisha chit chatted about various issues and topics.

At first Markus was jealous, listening to Tanisha and Sparks. They seemed to hit it off and were interested in the same sort of stuff. Markus thought he was the only one who could make Tanisha laugh to the point where her stomach ached, he wasn't. Sparks proved to be quite an interesting dude.

They had consumed more than enough alcohol by the time they left BBQ's. Trudging through the busy sidewalks of NYC, they readily followed Tanisha to wherever she wanted to shop. All she did was window shop.

Sparks was glad she didn't do more. He would have never done this with any female, including all of his babies' mothers. He was about ready to leave Markus and Tanisha's fat ass right there in the East Village. Tanisha looked at her watch and said, "I gotta meet a few of the girls at six in a lounge down in SOHO."

Sparks said, "What the fuck is a SOHO?"

She said, "Sparks, you don't get out much do you?"

"Only to go see my parole officer," Sparks deadpanned.

Markus laughed at what Sparks said. He knew Sparks had never been arrested in his life. A lot of dudes in the hood only left the hood for that particular reason.

"South of Houston Street," Tanisha explained. "It's another part of the Village. The lounge is mad cool. You'll be able to smoke your weed. They have an open area in the back with trees and benches. People go there to drink, smoke and listen to music."

"Sounds very entertaining," Sparks replied. "Are your friends white?"

Tanisha said, "You'll see."

"Are they from the job?" Markus asked.

Tanisha said, "You'll see."

Stepping inside the lounge, they went straight toward the back. It led outside, where there were trees and benches. A group of white people were over in a far corner talking, laughing, drinking, smoking cigarettes, and weed. Sparks inhaled and then smiled, welcoming the aroma.

He held out his hand in Tanisha's direction. She paused, giving him a queer look. Tanisha smiled, went in her purse, and handed the blunt to him. It was crooked. He scrutinized it for a beat then straightened it out and sparked the ganja.

"My friends are over there, I see them." She pointed.

Markus immediately saw the flawless specimen that presented him with glimpses of his past. She was the woman who made him black out every time he laid eyes on her. Saturday evening wasn't any different from any other day. There was Michelle. Markus began feeling lightheaded. He could hear Tanisha saying, "No, not again, Markus!"

"What the fuck is going on?" Sparks shouted while reaching out and grabbing Markus by the shoulder.

Sparks's fast reflexes prevented Markus from hitting the ground but he was loosing his hold on him. Sparks however lost his grip on the blunt he was smoking. Sparks had less than a second to decide whether to get a firmer grip on Markus or catch his blunt before it hit the ground…

When Markus woke from his blackout Saturday night at the lounge, Michelle was nowhere to be seen. She left as soon as he hit the ground. One of her friends, a woman named Kendra stayed. She knew who Markus was, he was Mr. Excitement. She was so humored by the whole situation, her best friend Michelle was sending the super porn star unconscious with a look. Kendra laughed at Michelle when Markus hit the floor and pointed at her and said, "Medusa. This is like that except no turning to stone. Zap!"

Tanisha told Markus once he was revived that Michelle found the whole thing bizarre and wasn't amused. She said, "Call her when you ain't retarded and explain yourself."

Nancy got a call from Markus around ten Sunday evening. He told her he had slept for more than twenty-four hours after their little date and that he had passed out once again upon sight of Michelle. Nancy asked him if he had taken any drugs or done anything out of the ordinary, and whether he was overly fatigued. He said no.

She was thinking about something Markus had said while typing away on her laptop in her apartment. He called their rendezvous a date. She wasn't so sure about calling it that, but dating a client was a no-no. Not to mention, all the porn movies she purchased and watched. She touched herself more than she did the first time she watched them. Nancy didn't know what to think. She had started thinking about Mr. Excitement way too much.

"If he has another one of those sleeping occurrences again," she said talking into a small microphone while typing. "I'll look into it more thoroughly. If he doesn't, I won't waste time on it."

Realizing that the more pressing issue was his blacking out, Dr. Adler had done research and gathered information. The psychiatrist knew that somehow she had to convince him that hypnosis, placing him under a subconsciously submissive state, seemed the only way to truly find out what was going on with him. She knew that Markus was not interested in hypnosis, but Dr. Adler wanted to know what was going on inside his skull, and what Michelle meant.

She had suspicions but had not spoken to Markus as much as she needed to. Monday evening would be very challenging. She had to convince Markus to accept hypnosis. She was growing physically fond of him. As she typed her notes, Nancy felt the freaky urge to put on one of Markus's movies. She was not able to totally concentrate on the well being of her patient. Nancy was fantasizing about Mr. Excitement sticking his dick inside of her.

Her phone rang. She knew who it was before she even picked

up the phone.

"Gary thanks for returning my call. I know it's late but I want you to come to my office tomorrow at around 8 pm... No, not for a job but for a potential one, I want you to talk to a patient of mine... About what, what do you think Gary, hypnosis, what else would it be...? No. Gary I can't reveal the nature of my patient's condition. That is for him to tell you but afterwards, if he agrees to the procedure I'll certainly give you all the details... Thanks Gary, see you tomorrow."

Monday morning Markus figured he would catch a cab. First his tires were slashed now the windows of his Lexus were smashed. The car had to be towed to the dealership for repairs. He didn't concern himself with his car situation for too long. He was always business first, everything else second.

Sparks was downstairs in front of Markus's building bright and early Monday morning on the hood of his car with a blunt dangling from the side of his mouth.

"Let me be your manager," Sparks said, exposing all his teeth. "We can't let a nigga like Cali slow us down," he added still exposing all his teeth.

"We," Markus uttered flabbergasted.

He hopped inside Sparks's car and they were off. Monday morning, bright and early, Markus stepped into the offices of Smut Central as his agent instructed him. She had called him at five a.m. waking him from his pleasant slumber so that he wouldn't be late.

Markus as usual had a very unusual weekend and was looking forward to his session with Nancy Adler. He had so much to share with her. Every time he suffered a blackout he was able to remember more of his past. All of that was in the back of his mind. Smut Central was now the important issue.

"Yo," Sparks worded passing the blunt he was smoking. Markus came back to reality as he grabbed the blunt. "Stop day dreaming. Any of those porn bitches gonna be here today?"

"I don't know," Markus said.

He gave the smoking narcotic a menacing look then gave his friend the same eyes.

"Did you read all the no smoking signs on your way up? And I mean from the building's hallway lobby, to the elevator and look over on that wall. What does that say?"

Sparks looked at the wall. They were in the waiting area. The secretary was occasionally glancing at them with disinterest since they arrived. She showed no real interest till Sparks lit his cigar wrapping filled with weed. Then she pressed a button on the intercom on her desk and mumbled something Markus couldn't hear.

Sparks said, "Sorry nigga. They should be specific about shit. It says no smoking but it doesn't say what you shouldn't smoke, I just assumed since weed was illegal they were referring to cigarettes. Why tell me not to smoke something I shouldn't be smoking anyway."

He gave Markus a huge grin and the secretary the same.

"Don't ruin this for me." Markus snapped.

He snatched the blunt from Sparks, took the blunt to a window, opened it and tossed it out. Sparks winced, mumbled and sat down. Sparks picked up a copy of Smut Central's magazine and became engrossed in it.

After a while the secretary said, "Tony Jersey will see you now, Markus Johnson."

"Good luck," Sparks worded with his head still in the magazine.

"Thanks," Markus returned to the secretary while frowning at Sparks.

"How's my star this morning?" Tee-Neck loudly greeted. It was seven in the morning and Markus didn't answer. He responded with a slight grin. "Have a seat."

Markus sat. Tee-Neck was a no-nonsense business type, but fair. He paid Smut Central employees well. Markus knew all he had to do was listen. This was the first time Tee-Neck wanted to see him without his agent present. "I'm gonna get straight to it," he began. "We love you here at Smut Central. We got big plans for you. Daisy Lace thinks you're the next big thing."

"What do you think?" Markus asked.

Tee-Neck leaned in over his desk and gave him the sternest leer.

"It never matters what I think, only what the money thinks. Your movies sell." He moved a dozen or so stapled papers across his desk. "Read this over carefully or get somebody else to."

Tony grabbed a cigar from the box of Cuban's on his desk. There was a Zippo lighter on the desk also, he grabbed that and lit the Cuban. After a few puffs and coughs he said, "Want one?"

"Why not," Markus answered, eyeing the stapled sheets of paper Tee-Neck pushed over to him. "What is this?"

"A contract," Tee-Neck coughed. "It's you and Smut Central Entertainment, an exclusive deal. Look at those numbers, six digits for one year." He rose from the desk with the box of cigars. Markus took one, put it in his mouth. Tee-Neck clipped the tip of the cigar and lit it for him. "Take this." The receding hair lined owner of Smut Central handed him a pair of airline tickets. "Sign the contracts and next month you are off to the Orient for your first real movie with Smut Central."

"Real movie... The Orient...?" Markus uttered confused. "Where...?"

"Japan, Mr. Excitement does Japan," Tee Neck wheezed as he laughed. "That is a script for another movie," he said, reaching for a folder on his cluttered desk and handing it to Markus.

"A fucking script...?" Markus asked incredulously.

"Yeah, it's more than fucking over here at Smut Central," he said, placing an arm around Markus's shoulders. "Go over those contracts. Call me in a couple of days. This is the big league, boy. This ain't five grand an ejaculation. This is health insurance with fucking dental."

Tee-Neck went back to his desk. He puffed more of his cigar while Markus sat, his own cigar burning unattended. Markus didn't puff. He stared at the boss of Smut Central who had just tossed him a six digit contract.

"That's it boy. Get the fuck out of my office." Markus stood and made his exit.

Markus and Sparks were about to leave when Vonchell slinked into the office. Vonchell was looking so ravishingly beautiful, Sparks totally forgot what he was about to ask Markus. She was wearing a leather bolero jacket and a very expensive looking, white sundress. She saw the guy with Markus studying her, so she spun around and said, "Tracy Reece."

Starting with her sandals, that had straps wrapped all the way up her exposed thighs, Sparks gave the sexy porn star all his attention.

"Hey Markus, how are you?" Vonchell sang.

"I'm great," Markus frowned at her. "Oh, this is a friend of mine, Sparks."

"Spark…"

"Hello Tracy Reece," Sparks said, extending a hand while lecherously eyeing her. "The name's Sparks."

Vonchell laughed, "The dress is Tracy Reese. But all of this," she said doing a twirl. "All of this is Vonchell."

"Let's go," Markus told Sparks.

Markus wasn't feeling Vonchell. She left directly after he blacked out in the restaurant. Tanisha and Entice told him that Vonchell wasn't remotely concerned about his health. All she wanted to do was leave.

"What's that in your hand?" Vonchell asked.

"My future, bitch," Markus barked.

"Oh, is that what it is. Hold on tight, Mr. Excitement. You have lost your past. You do not want to lose your future. If you do then all you'll have is the present," Vonchell laughed, walking into Tee-Neck's office.

Vonchell did not even glance at the receptionist. Sparks's eyes followed her all the way inside. His body would have followed her too, but Markus grabbed him by an arm, and dragged him down the hallway to the elevator.

At the elevator, Markus was pressing the button vigorously. He didn't give a damn about Vonchell. She was only a woman he fucked in a movie. Markus's thoughts were on the contract in his hand. Sparks grabbed the contract while they were in the elevator and flipped through it.

"Sign this," Sparks said in his best business tone. "Of course we gotta change a few things. My ten percent, it isn't anywhere in here. We gotta whip up a contract for our agreement."

"What?" Markus blurted, "Ten percent... Our agreement...?"

"Yeah, I ain't asking for much, some managers get, say fifteen or twenty," Sparks laughed. "Relax nigga. I trust that you'll pay my black ass accordingly."

Markus looked at him with a blank face. He couldn't tell if Sparks was joking. Sparks knew about his situation. They spoke a great deal since the tire slashing incident. Sparks said, "I see nothing about your agent in this contract."

Very observant, Markus thought, eyeing Sparks. Maybe he would make a good manager.

"I don't know what that means. Audra introduced me to Tee-Neck, and the whole Smut Central situation. Now it seems like she isn't even in the picture."

"Not so," he interjected. "She called you and informed you about this meeting, right?"

"True," he agreed. "Tee-Neck didn't mention Audra, and she

didn't come to the meeting. I guess there's a first time for everything. If you get my meaning…?"

"Perhaps," Sparks replied. "What now, nigga?"

When the elevator hit ground floor, Markus bumped into Entice. Another pretty girl caused Sparks to stop whatever he was saying. He stared lustfully at Entice. She was better looking than all his babies' mothers combined, and all the other dames he knew. She was on Tanisha's level but no where near the beauty of Vonchell. Still, she had a fat ass and was good looking enough to harass.

"And you are?" He asked Entice.

She ignored Sparks, "Hi Markus," she sang. "They called you in today?"

"Yeah, how you been Entice?"

Entice stayed the whole time during his black out incident at the restaurant. She rode in the ambulance with him. She even accompanied Tanisha and Markus home to make sure he was alright afterwards.

"I've been good. Tee-Neck called me the other day and told me to drop by the office. So early, I wasn't sure what he wanted."

She had to press the elevator button because as they began talking the door closed. The elevator was going up without her.

"You got a manager." Sparks asked her.

"Who is this dude?" She asked, finally acknowledging Sparks's existence.

"I'm his manager," Sparks said before Markus could respond. "Holla at me, don't sign those contracts until I thoroughly go over them."

Entice didn't know what he was talking about. She said, "Wait for me," to Markus. The elevator came back down and opened. She hopped in.

"I think I'm in love," Sparks smiled, taking an excessively long look at Entice's body before the elevator door closed.

Markus didn't want to wait for Entice, but Sparks insisted they did. It was his ride so Markus did not have much choice in the matter. Luckily the wait was over in twenty minutes. Her meeting with Tee-Neck lasted as short as Markus's.

Vonchell stepped out the building with Entice. They shared a few words and Vonchell walked away. Entice saw Markus and Sparks inside the car. They were in front of the building. She walked over and hopped in the backseat.

"I'm starving," she announced.

"Yeah, well maybe we can all get a bite to eat," Markus suggested.

"We gotta get your car. They should have towed it already. Call and find out when you can go get it. I got business to take care of," Sparks said.

He was quite sure Sparks had drug dealing business to handle. Markus figured Sparks hadn't been away from the hood this much in his whole drug dealing existence. It was only a matter of time before the streets started calling him. And hot looking women or not, he had to respond.

Entice and Markus spoke about their new contracts as they drove looking for somewhere to get breakfast. Entice was offered an exclusive deal with Smut Central though her deal wasn't as high powered as Mr. Excitement's. That didn't matter much to her. She knew her worth and figured she was worth exactly what they would pay her if she signed exclusively to Smut Central Entertainment.

Entice wasn't sure if she wanted to do that.

She never expected to spend much time fucking on film. Her first sex scene was with Markus and that was a week ago. She just needed some quick money and did not intend to make it a career.

Markus Johnson's situation was entirely different. He had nothing going in life but the porn industry. He didn't even have a real birth certificate, hadn't a confirmed identity. He did have a big dick. He was going to sign the contract. Entice didn't know what she was going to do.

15

After breakfast at a diner in midtown, Sparks dropped Markus off at the car dealership. His car was back to normal, looking the way it did before it was vandalized. Entice wanted to accompany Markus but Markus told her he had a few things to take care of. Sparks told Entice he would drop her wherever she wanted to go, or they could do something else. His eyes were gleaming with designs on getting better acquainted with her anatomy. She reluctantly agreed to do something else with him.

Markus's first line of business was to go see Tanisha. He hadn't spoken to her since he blacked out at the lounge Saturday night. At first Markus was angry at her for bringing him to the lounge and surprising him with Michelle. He didn't want to blackout the first time he was formally introduced to the woman. He did. Michelle was some sort of key to his past. He wouldn't be able to question her if he couldn't stay conscious around her.

Markus drove to Tanisha's. He figured he would have a much needed talk with her, visit with his daughter, then see Nancy Adler. Gwyneth was another issue entirely. It was always an issue he avoided. The last time he was around Gwyneth it was disastrous. She propositioned him for sex, he refused, and she thoroughly trashed her living room while he watched. Emily was very frightened, but not nearly as frightened as she was when he fainted.

He parked across the street from Tanisha's, hopped out the Lexus and saw a familiar vehicle parked in front of the building. It was Cali's car. "What the fuck is he doing here?" Markus mumbled.

The sight of Cali's car parked in front of Tanisha's angered him. Sparks mentioned that Tanisha and Cali had some connection. Tanisha never mention Cali in a conversation before and Cali never spoke of her. He didn't understand what was going on. But Markus knew exactly how much it cost to replace his tires and car windows. It was obvious that something fishy was going on. He hopped back inside the Lexus.

He sat in his vehicle thinking about what he was going to do next. Markus wanted to go upstairs and confront them. But where would that lead? He thought. Sparks had talked about Tanisha's activities inside the VIP room and that meant she was possibly still playing the role of a prostitute.

Markus was angrier at Tanisha than he was at Cali. All he wanted was for her to be the very best she could. He knew she was way better than sucking dicks. And Cali was nothing but trouble. "Who am I to judge anyone?" He said aloud. "I'm a damn porn star."

He decided to go upstairs. If anything, he would question Cali about the slashed tires. Sparks told him he didn't give a fuck about Cali and if he had beef with him he was prepared to ride. Cali was a drug dealer and the word out on the street told he wasn't beyond shooting someone. Markus had enough problems simply being him, a person without a past. He was about to step out his vehicle and walk upstairs to Tanisha's but his cell phone beeped.

"Audra…"

"How did the meeting go?" His agent asked.

"I don't know. Tee-Neck gave me a contract. Did you know he was gonna do that?" Markus asked.

"Of course not," she snapped with a touch of confusion. "Did you sign anything?"

"No. Do you wanna look over the contract?" He asked.

"I sure do. We don't have an escrow agreement Markus Johnson, but we do have a verbal one. Verbal agreements are binding and the courts recognize them…"

"Wait a minute, Audra," he interjected. He knew a threat when he heard it. "You didn't wanna give me a written contract because you didn't want anyone to know you had a porn star as a client…" Not that your B movie clients are any better than me. He thought.

"You're an adult entertainer," Audra broke in, sounding furious. "Fuck the preliminary shit. I got you where you are today. Before me you were fucking white trailer trash and fat black bitches with bullet wounds on their thighs and stretch marks all over their bodies."

"Simmer down Audra. I ain't crossing you. You'll get your ten percent."

"Ten," She scoffed. "I deserve more. How much did they offer you?"

"I think you should talk to my manager from now on. I don't like your tone of voice."

"Tone of voice…?" Audra sounded flabbergasted. "You

ungrateful, no good…"

He ended the conversation by flipping his cell phone shut. After laughing he opened the phone again. He typed Audra a text message telling her that everything was going to be alright, that they should schedule a meeting and talk things over. Markus laughed. His mind went back to where it was before she called. He looked across the street and saw that Cali's car was gone. Audra distracted him.

Cali left Tanisha's and drove off, from under his nose. He breathed in a great deal of air and let it out slowly. He was glad Cali left before he went inside. He wasn't anxious to confront him. He needed to talk to Tanisha first.

He usually gave her a call before he dropped by, not this time. He went inside her building and took the stairs. He usually knocked but rang the bell instead.

"Who is it?"

Markus stayed silent and waited. He figured she would look through the peephole, see him and immediately open the door. She didn't. She said, "Hold on." He waited. About four minutes later, she opened the door. He eyed her suspiciously. Tanisha was draped in one of her silk robes. He walked in, went to the living room and sat on the couch.

"I'm gonna take a shower," she mumbled.

"Don't bother, I ain't gonna be here long."

"You wanna drink?" She asked. "I got a bottle of wine in the fridge."

"I ain't gonna be here long," he snapped. "Cali was here. I didn't even know you knew him like that. Why was he here?"

"Why are you asking?" She responded with a lot of venom.

"The nigga slashed my tires and broke all my car windows."

"How can you be so sure?" She questioned. "Anybody could

have done that."

He gave her another set of sharp eyes. She was diverting her eyes from his and could barely look him in the face. A long moment of silence was between them. Markus got off the couch.

"Wait," Tanisha blurted. "It isn't what you think."

"What do I think?" He asked. "Please tell me?"

"Why are you even thinking? Why Mark you ain't my man! You wanna know why he was here? Don't you already know why?" Tanisha asked before her guilty disposition turned into anger.

"I guess I do," he said damn near whispering. "Why fuck around with him? The nigga is no good, probably only using you. The nigga fucked up my car. I told you that on Saturday."

"He means nothing to me. It's business, that's all it is Mark. I'm using him. Why do you even care?"

He didn't know what to say. Markus's mind was working overtime. He cared because he loved her he supposed. She wasn't his but at times it felt like she was. Markus didn't know what was going on. There were many mixed emotions circling around.

"Where did you meet Cali, in Jingling Babes?" He asked.

"Yes," she said with brutal honesty. "He wanted more than a look at my body and a lap dance. He has a lot of money. I have a need for more money."

He couldn't believe what he was hearing. He knew Tanisha was what she was. He met her during a porn shoot. He fucked her in front of the cameras moments after they were introduced. What did he expect from her? He didn't know. He felt wrong. Who was he to judge anyone?

"You promised me you wouldn't prostitute yourself anymore," Markus said.

"I gotta live, Markus."

He gave her a dirty look and she felt like vomiting. His expression made her sick. Markus always had a way of making her feel more the whore than she already felt. She thought it was because of the way he made her feel when he was inside of her. It wasn't entirely the size of his dick. She knew he cared and could see it in his eyes. All she saw in other men's eyes were reflection of her lips before she got on her knees.

She had been hurting herself her whole life and was familiar with the pain. She knew he meant well and didn't want to hurt him. Markus was her dear friend. She felt that she had betrayed him. He didn't know her as well as he had thought. She could never be the sort of girl he wanted her to be.

"I think you better leave."

She couldn't believe what she said. Cali wasn't half the person Markus was. He wasn't worth much. Tanisha was caught up. She couldn't tell Markus the bitter truth though she was certain he knew enough already. Cali and his cronies started muscling in on the owner of Jingling Babes. Cali fancied himself a pimp. He was always with a lot of rough looking dudes. They flashed pistols in situations where a normal pimp would only need the pimp psychology, and the baby powdered hand.

She didn't have the guts to tell Markus, Cali had forced her to be his number one hooker. She gave Markus the blankest face she could. She was a bottom ho now. Markus didn't say anything until he got to the door.

"I thought what we had was more than this. I'm not sure now. I know why I do what I do…If you get my meaning…? But I saw so much in you. You always had a choice."

"Life is full of choices. Sometimes we make the wrong ones and sometimes we are forced to do things we don't wanna. You think

Cali is using me," she said with an evil laugh. She was trembling and crying inside. "I'm using him. I'm a man eater. I was using you too. I just didn't gobble you whole."

After Markus left Tanisha locked her door and said, "What we had was more than the world, Mark. I never used you."

She broke out in tears. Her body slid to the floor. She stayed on the floor curled in the fetal position for hours. Eventually she stood, walked into her bathroom and prepared for her shower. Before she slipped out of her robe she looked at her face in the mirror. "When I look at myself I see nothing but a prostitute. I love you, Mark. But I can't see myself through your eyes. I only see me through this mirror."

16

Markus was in a somber mood when he left Tanisha's apartment. He thought he knew her better. "I guess I was wrong," he worded as he walked to the car. He figured in a couple of days, she would call him, and they would straighten things out.

In the meantime he decided to gather some additional information on Cali. Markus was certain that Sparks could provide the additional information. He didn't want to get into any street stuff with Cali. His life was complicated enough as it was without street stuff.

"I can't concentrate on this. I gotta go see my daughter."

He pulled out from where he parked and made his way to Manhattan. He hoped Gwyneth was in a better mood than she was after he refused to have sex with her on Thursday. He was too preoccupied with his own thoughts to notice anything but the road in front of him.

He didn't see the car following. The driver kept his distance, always two or three cars behind the Lexus. Cali was on the passenger side, one of his cronies was behind the wheel.

"Keep out of sight, nigga," Cali said. "We're gonna see what's poppin for the porn star tonight."

"Why?" A far more curious crony in the back seat asked.

Cali narrowed his eyes before answering the dude. He wasn't used to being questioned by anybody, but he was in a good mood. Earlier Tanisha had done an excellent job of sucking his dick.

"Why, you say. Because…"

That was enough for his cronies. The driver kept his distance, staying within sight of the Lexus and continued to follow.

Gwyneth's husband was a very successful entrepreneur. He started out working in the mailroom of a small stockbrokerage firm as a clerk, eventually became a stockbroker and after a lot of success left the firm to start his own, Manners Brokerage.

After a decade of more downs than ups, Manners Brokerage became a very competitive brokerage firm. By the age of thirty-five, Mr. Manners had managed to become a millionaire and his company was grossing multi-millions by the time he hit forty.

Gwyneth married Mr. Manners for his wealth, and because of his poor health. He suffered from many afflictions even before he was diagnosed with a rare bone disease. He was impotent by the time he hit thirty, and restricted to a wheelchair one year after.

Gwyneth was eighteen years old, and a sophomore in college when she met him. She was stunningly beautiful, and far from innocent. She saw a goldmine the moment she spotted Jonathan Jacob

Manners at an economics seminar held at the university she attended.

She was an economics major and Jonathan Manners was known to her. Everyone in the economics department knew who he was. Although most didn't know he was confined to a wheelchair, and in such a fragile state of health, until he made one of his rare appearances.

It mattered little to Gwyneth. She made sure that she sat in the front row where he couldn't miss her. Gwyneth made sure she crossed her length of bare legs and that he got a good look at what wasn't under her short skirt. Jonathan had taken a long glance at her while he was at the podium. He couldn't keep his eyes off her. She knew she had him exactly where she wanted him.

He wasn't the first man Gwyneth used. He was the first one she looked at with dollar signs. They courted for a half year. She would wheel him to the park where they would sit and talk economics and politics. For Gwyneth being in public with Jonathan Manners was an embarrassment. But it was all an elaborate plot. The ends would eventually justify the means.

Jonathan inevitably asked for her hand in marriage and Gwyneth accepted. Things were going according to her plans. He married her with no prenuptial. All she had to do was jerk her husband's dick while he sat in his wheelchair. She would jerk him for hours. He was always flaccid, could never get a full erection.

Although he still had an urge for sex, no blood flowed through his penis. Eventually things migrated to him liking to see his young beautiful wife getting fucked by other men. In the beginning, Gwyneth was completely against it, but eventually she conceded. Jonathan might have been physically weak but he was mentally sound. Gwyneth loved sex and she couldn't get it from her feeble husband. She also suffered from manic depression.

Jonathan used this to his advantage. The drugs she took were drugs his personal physician prescribed. Gwyneth was constantly under medication. Jonathan always had a few of his young male friends over. Gwyneth found herself being taken by three to four men at a time. She was so medicated she couldn't remember what was going on. Jonathan loved to watch his lovely wife getting fucked.

Now thirty-nine years old, Gwyneth harbored many sexual preferences, fetishes, fantasies and perversions. She wasn't sure if they were genuinely formulated from the kinkiness she endured being Mrs. Gwyneth Manners or if she was a freaky thing beforehand.

She loathed her husband. When she was eighteen years old, she figured she would outlive her husband three or four times over. She figured that when he passed away she would still be young and have plenty of time to enjoy all the money. He managed to hold on to life longer than she planned and even longer than any of his doctors anticipated.

The phone rang as Gwyneth was in the middle of her midday workout. She was on the Stairmaster machine in the gym.

"What is it?" Gwyneth snapped.

"Someone is here to see you," the doorman said. "It's Markus Johnson."

"Let him up," she said pressing a button on the cordless phone, and tossing it. "Valencia!" she shouted at the top of her lungs, calling the maid.

"Yes, Mrs. Manners," Valencia said after she ran into the room.

She seemed more out of breath than Gwyneth, like she had done twenty virtual flights. Gwyneth and Jonathan Manners lived in a three story penthouse apartment.

"Markus is here. Is Emily awake?" She asked.

"No, Mrs. Manners. She's still napping."

Valencia had a heavy Sicilian accent. She was a young, slim, shapely, olive complexioned auburn haired beauty. She was always adorned in a black and white maid's uniform. It was the tightest and shortest skirt uniform Gwyneth could find. She liked Valencia very much.

"Send Markus here."

She dismissed the maid with a wave of a hand. She still had another fifteen minutes on the Stairmaster before her workout was finished. She was thinking about a different sort of workout when Markus walked into the gym.

"Where's Emily?" Markus asked as soon as he walked in.

"She's taking a nap and don't you dare disturb her," she said walking flights. "We got off on the wrong foot the last time you came over."

"I guess we did, Gwyneth," he said dryly.

"Call me what you used to call me."

"Bitch, I used to call you bitch, and things worse."

"You used to call me your white thang. Don't you remember that? You were younger and stupider. I guess you think you're smart and independent now. You still need me," she said, breathing hard.

"What do I need you for? Money...? A place to stay...? What...? Why do I still need you?"

Her eyes widened like silver dollars. "You signed complete and utter guardianship of Emily to me and Jonathan," she laughed menacingly. "You don't even have visitation rights. I let you see her out of the kindness of my heart. I would say you need me a great deal."

"What do you want?" He asked.

"Your big, black dick..."

Markus began unbuckling his belt. He let his jeans drop to his construction boots. "You want this?" He asked, reaching inside his boxers. "This is what you want? I'm supposed to keep fucking you. Haven't you had enough?"

"Suppose I haven't...? So many questions Markus," she said, turning off the machine.

Gwyneth grabbed the towel draped on the handle bars, stepped off the virtual stairs. She stood in her tight spandex shorts with her sports bra, dripping with sweat, looking good.

"So many questions..."

She was once someone he looked forward to seeing when he was young and naïve. Now he hated the sight of the woman and wouldn't mind seeing her dead.

Gwyneth once kept Markus from seeing Emily for eight months. During that time Markus didn't know what to do and felt like committing suicide. Emily was all the family he had. His daughter was the only certainly tangible thing he had.

Markus moved on Gwyneth in a burst of rage, forcefully grabbing her by her long blonde hair. He yanked her to the floor as Gwyneth cried out in pain. Savagely Markus pulled down her spandex shorts and realized how much she was enjoying the roughhousing. Her pussy glistened and bubbled. Gwyneth was looking up into his face, her eyes twinkling.

"Yes," she purred. "Pretend I'm a slave master's wife, like old times."

He didn't want to see her face and vehemently turned Gwyneth over on her stomach. Markus knew how she loved looking into his face, but all he wanted to do was fuck her as hard and deeply as he could. Not out of passion or lust, but anger and hatred.

He speared her soft walls with his hard dick, for what seemed like forever to him. Markus wanted her to explode. He didn't want to be inside her for long. He kept her face down on the floor, mashed her face so hard her nose started bleeding. She was having the hardest time breathing but she was enjoying every moment of the conflict and pain.

She was squirming, attempting to move her body away from the thick shaft working in and out of her. Violently with only a few grunts, he fucked Gwyneth. She tried crawling away from the pleasurable pain, but Markus wouldn't have it. He used both hands to press down on her shoulder blades, preventing her from turning around or rising.

Gwyneth was helpless and screaming loudly. Markus kept inflicting painful thrusts.

"I'm coming…!" she screamed.

Her body lost all its strength. She ceased struggling and started her whimpering. She had reached her climax and Markus immediately released his grip. He got up, pulled up his pants, and went to a window. He stood there looking outside.

A couple minutes later, Gwyneth turned over. She stood on wobbly legs as Markus eyed her in disgust. Blood leaked from one of her nostrils and Gwyneth's eyes glinted with light. She enjoyed it. Gwyneth staggered over to a table and grabbed a lighter and a cigarette.

"Shit, you practically raped me," she coughed, smiling.

"I was trying to kill you. Can I see Emily now?" Markus uttered with indifference.

"I suppose you can," she sang, taking a long pull on the cigarette. "You didn't cum."

He walked out the room without saying anything to her. Markus wanted to see his daughter, take a shower, and see his shrink.

He didn't get a chance to spend much time with Emily. She was sleeping so soundly he did not want to wake her. Markus watched her snoring softly in her bed. Emily was beautiful and precious. She was his blood, his daughter. He kissed her softly on her cheek.

Markus took a shower, washing the foul scent of Gwyneth off him. She was somewhere in the penthouse apartment. She got what she wanted from him. After showering, Markus left. The maid showed him to the door. Markus knew every inch of the apartment and didn't need her assistance on the way out.

"What the fuck!" He exclaimed once downstairs.

It was all he could say. He was looking out the front entrances window. He parked a half block from the building. He walked out the building's revolving door, saw his car in the distance and ran over to it. All of his tires had been slashed.

Markus looked around suspiciously. It was a little after five in the evening. His appointment with his shrink was at six. He didn't want to miss his session with Nancy Adler. Markus was confused and angry.

"Did you do this, Cali?" He speculated loudly to no one.

Emily and Gwyneth had been Markus's best kept secret. He thought about Tanisha then shrugged the thought off, hailed a yellow cab and hopped in. He called Gwyneth and told her about his vehicle. Markus asked her to handle things for him.

He muttered a curse after he got off the phone. Gwyneth always expected to be repaid whenever she did him a favor. She was more than happy to take care of Markus's car situation.

He called Sparks and told him about his car incident. Sparks listened and after hearing all the details said, "We are gonna handle this, tonight."

Sparks hung up the phone before Markus could say anything. He cursed under his breath. Markus didn't feel like handling anything tonight. All he wanted to do was go see his shrink and go to sleep.

When he stepped into Nancy's office, Markus was very distressed. Marching into the office and ignoring the secretary.

"No need to knock Mr. Johnson, come on in," Nancy said sarcastically.

"Sorry," he said meekly. Markus sat on the couch. "My life is getting worse."

"In what way…?" She asked. She sat on the chair that was always adjacent to the couch. "How has your life gotten worse?"

"This guy is antagonizing me. He's stalking me," he began

then changed directions. "Fuck that! We can get into that later. On a
brighter note, I haven't had a black out since the last one I told you
about."

"That's good news," Nancy said. "Have you been thinking
about this woman Michelle much? Is it because you've been blocking
her out?"

"I've got a lot on my mind. I think it's my other situations.
I got a contract from the company I work for. They offered me an
exclusive deal with them. It's a six figure deal."

"Good for you, Markus, congratulations."

"Don't congratulate me. I don't really wanna do porn for the
rest of my life," he said sadly. "Signing will keep me in the circuit for
a year, and that year will turn into a few more years. I need the money.
I don't have any other choice. If you get my meaning…?"

"You have your whole life ahead of you. You're twenty years
old." Nancy changed the direction of the conversation abruptly. "I've
been studying the nature of things, and haven't exactly come up with
a single concrete thing that could aid you, besides hypnosis." She
saw the way his face scrunched up. "I want you to hear me out first,
Markus. And I want you to speak with a friend of mine."

"You've been talking about me to people?" He asked in a
suspicious tone.

"No. I have a friend named Gary Zimmerman. He's a private
investigator, more importantly he's one the best hypnotist in the
country. He could help you a great deal, Markus."

"I ain't feeling this, Dr. Adler."

"Michelle, Michelle, Michelle…" Nancy said all of a
sudden.

"What are you doing? Are you crazy…?"

The room began to engulf him. He felt the air being sucked

out from the office as it grew smaller. Markus began to gasp and the walls moved in, bottling him in.

"I can't breathe," he said struggling desperately. "There are other children in the room with me…! Flies, flies, all over…"

"What room?" Dr. Adler asked, examining Markus's fearful expression.

He attempted to rise from the couch while struggling to remain conscious. He was able to stand but crumpled to the floor. Baffled Dr Adler looked at Markus' body lying unconscious at the foot of the couch.

Gary had jokingly suggested the technique when he called her earlier. He was fishing for information on Markus. She refused to give him any additional information but did mention a certain woman who might possibly be the trigger to the black outs and flashbacks.

"Say her name a few times, like in that horror flick, *Candy Man*. See what happens," Gary said, laughing.

Gary Zimmerman would be at her office around eight. His joke was no longer a joke. Saying the name over and over did have an effect on Markus. Dr. Adler could not foresee her patient responding in this peculiar manner. Markus was completely blacked out just on the suggestion of the stimuli.

Markus awoke an hour later with a roaring headache. He was back on the couch. He remembered hitting the soft carpet when he fell. In spite of things, the carpet was a welcome when compared to his head hitting the edge of a table or while driving on the Brooklyn Bridge. He glanced at Nancy, sitting on her chair, studying him. He leered. She gave him a glass of water. He quickly drank the liquid.

"How long was I out?" Before the doctor could answer, Markus glanced at the clock on the wall. "Damn, I was out for an hour?"

"Yes," Dr. Adler confirmed. "Did you have another flashback?"

"I did. Two actually or it was one all jumbled with the man, woman, and that little girl, the children, the flies and the room."

"You were saying something about children, flies, and a room. Let's talk about this. You mentioned over the phone your flashbacks are beginning to last longer and you are able to see more. What exactly do you see?"

"I saw what I dreamt when I slept for twenty-four hours. I saw a man. He was dragging me away from the two people and the girl. He dragged me to a van, forced me inside and other kids were inside the van. Then I was in a room. There were so many children and uncountable flies, if I would have opened my mouth, they would have flown inside and gone into my stomach."

"Hmm, sounds really bizarre. Dreams are often like that. Was it scary, like a nightmare?"

"The man who dragged me away from the people was scarier than the room filled with the children, and flies. He was really creepy-like with a scar on his face. It twisted from his forehead to his chin. I saw him clearer than I've seen any person in all of these flashbacks. If you get my meaning…?"

"Do you still think the people you see are your parents?"

"I can't be real sure of that, they were smiling, but I know it felt like I was being kidnapped. The little girl was crying and the man and the woman were waving and smiling. Maybe they are my parents. Who knows? The man was white, aging, his hair line receded. If I saw a picture of him, I would be able to identify him. If I saw him in the street I would know who he was. All the kids in the room were scared of him."

"Let's talk about this room and the children. Do you know where this room is located?" She asked.

"What do you mean by that?" He asked, without being sure what she was getting at.

"Was it a room within a house, a building, or was it an orphanage?"

"I don't know," Markus said, still weak and woozy.

He got a good look at the doctor. With so many things weighing him down, Markus didn't realize how nicely Nancy Adler was dressed. It was sexy in a conservative sort of way, business skirt suit, black shirt, sand cream tie and her black jacket was on a hanger in her closet. Anything the doctor wore made her sexy since she had coke bottle curves. He smiled.

This time he could see that she indeed wore a garter. Her skirt was shorter and she was wearing black stockings. The garter held them up with clips and he saw the strap going up her thickness, her thighs.

"I love your legs," Markus uttered almost absentmindedly.

"Pardon me," she said, pretending he didn't say what she heard him say.

The intercom buzzed. She got up from her seat and scurried to her desk, "Yes?"

"Gary Zimmerman is here." The secretary answered.

"He's early," Nancy snapped. "I'll be with him in a minute."

She turned her attention to Markus. He was standing. She didn't want him to walk out. Dr. Adler knew she was pushing things by inviting Gary over, but only wanted to help Markus.

"It's ok," Markus uttered with a frown. "Invite this Gary fella in," He produced a sly grin.

"Are you sure?" she questioned not wanting to offend him.

Was he toying with her? Nancy Adler wondered. She heard his words coming through loud and clear.

"Let's see what he has to say. He can't do any worse for me than you did with that little trick." Markus said, watching her jaw drop. He laughed. "Go ahead and greet him, invite him in." He coldly told her before she could touch the intercom on the desk. She turned toward him, inquisitively. "I wanna see you walk. Your walk excites me."

"Does it now?" She asked daringly.

"It does. Women generally don't excite me because sex is work, not pleasure. When I look at you, I don't see work. If you get my meaning…?"

"Well Markus Johnson, I'm working and when I look at you, I see a client. I don't appreciate your behavior. I have not one iota of interest in you other than wanting to help you with your dilemma. I suggest you conduct as professionally as you can. Is that understood?"

"Yes. Sorry doctor."

Markus almost felt ashamed, damn near breaking down right under the scrutinizing gaze of the doctor. He watched her hips sway as she walked to the door. He saw Nancy look back, wanting to see if he was gawking. She caught him red handed. He saw her lips form a sneaky grin. She hastily turned her head. Nancy playfully bent a little while opening the door. She touched one of her upper calves, a bit of her skirt went up. He saw her casually snap the strap of her garter. The door closed behind her.

18

There were no overwhelming or distinguishing features, he was modestly dressed. Gary Zimmerman was a plain looking dude. His hair was medium length and dangled like it hadn't seen a comb in days. His shoes looked expensive but worn. He had on dark blue slacks, light blue buttoned shirt with a light blue tie haphazardly hanging from his neck not touching his shirt.

He arrogantly sat on Nancy's chair, went into the briefcase he carried, and pulled out a bottle of Jack Daniels.

"This divorce is driving me up the wall." He told no one in particular.

"This is the guy who's gonna help me with my problems," Markus laughed.

Markus began pacing the expanse of the wide bookshelf and then traveling back toward the door. Nancy thought Markus was going to walk out the session. He didn't.

"This guy looks like one of your clients, Nancy. What good is he gonna be?"

"Nancy is it, Dr. Adler." Gary said with a snicker turning from the bottle to give her his set of eyes. "How interesting," he then directed his attention toward Markus. He immediately saw the attraction between Nancy and Markus. It mattered little to him but Gary made note of it. He had never before heard any of Nancy Adler's patients call her by her first name. Gary held the bottle of Jack high offering it to Nancy's patient.

Gary Zimmerman was a fifteen year veteran of the NYPD. He was a highly decorated detective who was now retired and running his own private investigation agency. He saw more with a glance than most people could see with infra red binoculars in the dark. He learned a great deal about Markus already but had nothing to judge him on yet.

"Damn!" Markus gasped, shaking his head saying no to the offered bottle. He looked over at Nancy. "Damn!" he repeated emphatically.

Knowing the drinking was more Gary Zimmerman's stage performance than drowning misery from a divorce proceeding, though he indeed was going through a very disgusting divorce, Nancy laughed. Gary was an alcoholic but he never walked into her office with a bottle of Jack Daniels.

"Looks can be quite deceiving. Gary Zimmerman is an accomplished hypnotist, one of the best private investigators in the city and a bit of an actor."

"Well," Markus said, extending a hand to a seated Gary. "If this is an act, I must applaud you for doing a hell of a job. I was more than convinced you're an alcoholic."

Gary rose from the chair and returned the handshake.

"Some of the best roles are the ones being played off the silver screen," he said, gazing into Markus's eyes. "Yes," He said to Nancy without looking at her. "He has been under the stopwatch or penlight before. I would say I'm going to have a task ahead of me. It looks like the work of an expert."

"What…?"

Both Nancy and Markus exclaimed in unison. Markus shook off Gary's comment before the doctor.

"I only agreed to hear you out. I didn't say anything about being a task for anyone," Markus said.

"After you hear what I have to say. You'll be begging me to deprogram you."

"Deprogram…?" Nancy uttered.

Markus sat on the couch and explained his dilemma. Gary sat on the adjacent chair, listening while taking swigs from the bottle of Jack Daniels. Nancy looked and listened from her desk.

She was amazed at how well Markus explained his situation and even more amazed at Gary's interest. It was way past ten at night, far beyond the time she thought this first meeting between the two of them would take. Soon Gary began asking a lot of questions, asking Markus things Nancy chastised herself for not thinking of asking. She yawned. Nancy Adler was tired. She saw Markus yawn after she did, that made them laugh.

"I think I've heard enough." Gary Zimmerman said, with a raised eyebrow. "I think I can help you. I won't guarantee anything. This man with the scar on his face, this intrigues me more than anything else. I think I know who he is."

He saw Markus's and Nancy's eyes widen and held a hand up, halting any further bewilderment. "I refuse to speak on it now. I need to contemplate things." He stared at Markus. "You are in something far deeper than being expertly hypnotized."

There was a long pause. Markus and Nancy stared at each other. Suddenly things were beginning to unravel. Gary Zimmerman's raspy voice broke the silence.

"For starters, I think I can have you recount a great deal of the missing pieces under hypnosis. I can help you with the spells of blacking out and the weird dreams you've been experiencing. I can also help you find out your true identity. I doubt your birth name is Markus Johnson. This stinks of something I've known about for some time. When I was on the force they removed me from an investigation involving children being used as guinea pigs and being severely hypnotized."

Markus thought about hypnosis, it made his bones shiver, but the former detective mentioned something about an old investigation involving children being hypnotized.

"Why would someone hypnotize children?" Markus asked.

"So that the child won't be able to speak… Hypnotism can be used to reveal but it can also be used to hide. An expert can wipe away portions of your past or completely and utterly wipe out your mind," Gary told Markus.

"Uh… What…?"

"I know it sounds bizarre but look at you. You told me you can only remember as far back as this orphanage. You said it was like you woke up and were there, like that is where your life began."

"True," Markus said. After a slight pause, "How much is all of this gonna cost?" He decided to talk about something more tangible, money.

He wasn't sure if he wanted this guy prying into his head but he had no other choices. Zimmerman, still drinking from that bottle, was probably going to cost him a fortune. Nancy was correct in saying it was an act because once they began talking the drinking seemed not to have mattered.

"The hypnosis is part of your psychiatry sessions. You'll only be required to pay Mr. Zimmerman for his other services," Nancy said.

Her smile disarmed Markus. He was more open to the hypnosis intervention. Markus's curiosity had been revved.

"What other services? What more would I want from him besides stopping the blackouts?"

"I'm also a private investigator. How about wanting to know who you are, who your parents are?" Gary Zimmerman said. He focused his sight on Markus and continued. "Once I successfully deprogram these psychic blocks, you will remember. This will no doubt compel you to want to find out more. Such as, who you truly are and why these things were done to you."

"I'll see you two next Monday," Markus said and stood.

"No Markus, you will see us Wednesday. I don't want you passing out again. I think Gary should start as soon as possible."

"Why so soon…?" Markus asked.

"It's the most logical decision. I'll explain the whole process. Maybe you can read this *Hypnosis for Dummies* book I got here in my briefcase."

"I'll get the rundown on Wednesday." Markus said with a frown.

He walked to the door and a dizzying spell hit him as he was about to open the door. Lightheadedness overwhelmed him. Feeling like he was going to blackout again, Markus paused. All he wanted to do was leave.

"I'll see you Wednesday at eight sharp." Nancy said.

Markus waved and closed the door behind him. Cautiously he walked out the office and passed the secretary.

19

Markus stood in front of the building. All the things he learned today had his mind boggled. He was more confused with the clues about his situation than when he had no clues at all. Markus finally noticed that a light drizzle had started. A hand touching his shoulder roused him from his rumination.

"Do you need a lift somewhere?"

He heard the voice and Markus turned to see Gary Zimmerman.

"Yeah, I guess I do," Markus answered.

There was a horn honking coming from across the street. Markus saw Sparks in his car waving at him.

"I guess you don't," Zimmerman said, holding a hand out.

"Thanks Gary," Markus said, shaking his hand.

"You look like you could use a drink. Take this," Gary said.

He handed Markus the half empty bottle of Jack Daniels and walked away. Markus absentmindedly took the bottle. What the hell? He thought and took a swig. He expected to feel the heat and fire of the alcohol going down his throat. He didn't. All he tasted was ginger ale. He laughed as he walked across the street.

Nancy saw Markus hop inside the car across the street. She saw Gary walking down the block to his car parked on the corner.

"Wait," she shouted, jogging toward Gary.

"Need a lift, Nancy?" He asked.

"No, I need a few explanations."

"What needs to be explained? I thought—"

"You said something about a past case," Nancy said, cutting him off. "A case involving children being hypnotized...?"

"Yeah and..."

"You also said you think you know who the man in Markus' flashbacks is. How do you know all of this?"

"I did say those things, didn't I?" Zimmerman said, jostling in his pockets for car keys.

"Don't play games with me. I know you far too well. You are walking way too straight for a man who just drank half a bottle of liquor."

"You really like this Markus guy?" He asked.

Nancy's eyes opened wide and Zimmerman laughed. He opened the driver's side door.

"When I had just made detective back in the mid eighties, I was on the missing persons division. They couldn't make heads or tails out of most of the cases. Hundreds were kids reported missing daily. One particular missing person's case hit the media big. We jumped on it with urgency. Nothing came up that led us to the missing child. But the investigations led my partner and me to an orphanage. The orphanage boarded over two dozen children, six being special children who were reported missing for about two years. They all were about the same age, ten or twelve, boys and girls. The special ones did not recollect who they were or how they got to the orphanage."

"That's just crazy," Nancy Adler said.

The rain slowly turned into a downpour. Nancy didn't seem to notice. "What do you mean by special? Do you mean mentally challenged."

"I suppose so. But not the way you think. The six special boys and girls were apparently sexually molested, sodomized and worse. They had no knowledge of the events taking place. The whole investigation was crazy. We were tipped off by an anonymous phone call that led us to this orphanage in a remote part of Long Island."

"I'm not getting the gist of all of this, the connection—"

"The orphanage's staff was not present when we went to investigate. Only the children were there. They had been in the house for days without any supervision. The faculty mysteriously vanished. The NYPD wanted to turn the case over to the feds, but I couldn't let things go. Something inside the orphanage disturbed me more than the missing faculty and abandoned children."

"What?" Nancy asked eagerly.

"A pocket watch," he laughed. "With the initials F.R.R engraved on it. One of the special children was carrying it. But the kid didn't know who he was, much less where he acquired the watch. There was no additional DNA on the watch, no other fingerprints. All of the special ones were minority and black and all of them couldn't be identified. There were no records of their existence. The other children were from low income families, and parents with substance abuse issues. We found child abuse cases, and kids given up for adoption since birth, others reported as runaways. The FBI took over the investigation because of the six special children."

"I'm so lost, Gary."

"And so were we. The special children's psyches had been tampered with. I gathered this the moment I began talking to them. It was only a theory and no one wanted to go there with me. Even my partner thought I was crazy. The psychiatrists assigned to the case, wrote it off as amnesia due to their specific traumatic ordeals. I had never heard of a case of mass amnesia in my life. And beyond the ordeal all six of these kids had no knowledge of anything other than the orphanage. It was like their lives began there. Just like Markus." He laughed. "It's funny. They removed me from the case because I was getting too emotionally involved. Fritz Roy Randleman is a childhood hero of mine. He's the reason for my interest in hypnosis, the mystical arts and my card tricks."

"Fritz Roy Randleman…? The name is familiar," she uttered with confusion. "The initials on the watch, he was the man with the scar wasn't he?"

"I believe so. Because of this illusion he did with flies, he's known as, Lord of the Flies. It's a very impressive trick. No one knows how he does it. No one knows how he did a lot of the tricks. Randleman was very amazing. Some say he's a genuine warlock, a master of the black art. Markus's dream consisted of flies and the six special kids spoke of flies and were very frightened of them. I know it sounds weird, but what isn't weird about Markus. And the fact of the matter is this, after all of these years, the investigation left us just as clueless as the children we rescued. None of the faculty at the orphanage could be found and those we identified wound up dead once we got a positive lead on their whereabouts."

"So strange…" she uttered as the rain came.

"The orphanage did exist. And those children's minds were

wiped clean. Nancy, you tossed something at me that's been eating me to the bone for years. Randleman has been missing for years. It's like he vanished from the face of the earth. One moment he was the biggest thing since David Copperfield, the next he disappeared without a trace. All of the case's records went with the FBI. I heard from a source that they eventually got destroyed," Zimmerman took a deep breath before he hopped into the driver's side. "Get in, let me drive you home."

"I will if you promise to tell me some more," Nancy said.

Her eyes were dancing with curiosity as she hastily walked over to the passenger side. She hurriedly opened the door, and got in.

Markus couldn't help but be surprised when he saw who was in the back seat of Sparks's vehicle. He eyed Entice suspiciously as she casually waved at him.

"What's she doing here?" Markus asked.

"What does it look like she's doing? She's sitting in the backseat of my car."

After checking his rearview and side mirrors, Sparks drove off. He merged into traffic, glanced at Markus before speaking.

"I did some asking around in the hood and I'm positive that it's Cali. He's the one fucking around with your whip. We can handle him tonight. I know where he is," Spark said, looking at Markus.

"Where…?" he uttered before he came to his senses and said. "Handle what? How are we gonna handle him?"

Sparks nudged his jaw toward the glove compartment while he drove. Markus figured he wanted him to look in it. He opened it.

"Fuck!" he exclaimed. There was a gun in the glove compartment. "What are we gonna do with that?"

"Not we, you, nigga," Sparks said with a bit of heat. "I'm your manager, not your bodyguard, or some sort of stooge."

Sparks nodded his head reassuringly. Markus grimaced. He still wasn't sold on the management idea. He thought it was a joke with a terrible punch line. Markus stared at Sparks and looked at the gun in the glove compartment. It suddenly dawned on him that Sparks wasn't joking.

"That nigga slashed your tires twice. And he broke your windows. Cali's been following you around like some motherfucking stalker, homey."

Markus was about to respond, but Sparks beat him to the punch.

"It's only gonna get uglier. Cali's a crazy dude, but he is also bitch ass… Always doing dirt with a bunch of other niggas round him… Or he gets other niggas to do shit for him. You gotta set it on his ass. He's the sort of dude who won't understand talking. You gotta get at him like that."

"Get at him like how? Shoot him; kill him?" Markus asked, heatedly.

Sparks laughed, "Nah, nigga. I know you're a lover, not a fighter. Besides that you're my new commodity and my black ass wouldn't want to see your ass physically harmed. You gotta do something. Scare the nigga, or it's gonna only get worse. Pistol-whip his ass, fire off a few… Have his ass running. I don't know nigga. You just gotta do something. How many more times your black ass gonna get your car fixed, huh?"

"There's more to this, Markus. You'll be better off seeing shit with your own eyes. Sparks knows what he's talking about," Entice added.

Markus turned around glaring. He looked at her for a few beats before he finally asked, "What the fuck do you know about all this?"

"It's about to go down tonight. I know that for sure," Entice answered.

Sparks laughed and the grimace on Markus's face tightened. He was quite sure Entice was right. Something probably was going down tonight. Markus scratched his bald head because he wasn't sure what.

20

They drove to Jingling Babes. Markus figured he shouldn't have been as shocked as he was. He knew whatever was going down tonight, involved Tanisha. Questions came to his mind but Markus stifled them. He said nothing. He already knew. Cali was in Jingling Babes.

Pouring rain had calmed to drizzling as Sparks drove them to the destination then began pouring rain again. The precipitation worsened. Sparks complained because he recently had the car washed. He found a place to park and pulled in, still complaining he shut the engine off and took the keys out of the ignition. They all hopped out the car. Markus neglected to take the pistol out the glove compartment but while they were walking, Sparks nudged him with an elbow and slipped the gun into one of his jacket pockets.

"I don't want it," Markus said sternly. "I'm not gonna pistol whip or shoot Cali or anybody else. I got enough problems. If you get my meaning…?"

"Cool," Sparks said. "You know the owner of this club, don't you?"

Markus nodded.

"Well then, you can get the gun inside the club for me. Call the owner and have him meet us outside so we can walk in without being searched."

"Shit!" Markus exclaimed. "You have this all planned out, don't you?"

"Yup…!" Sparks answered. "You want your car going to the shop two or three times a week for the rest of your life?"

"Maybe I should tell the authorities…" Markus began.

"Your black ass ain't gonna tell the cops, like you some little bitch ass?" Sparks interjected.

A long cold stare followed Sparks's scalding words. Markus had the meanest look he could muster.

"Don't call a nigga with a gun in his pocket a little bitch ass, it ain't healthy. If you get my meaning…?"

"Now that's what the fuck I wanna hear. Now you're talking my language."

"Call the owner," Entice urged.

"Why do you wanna be around all this bullshit? Don't you have anything better to do?" Markus asked, giving her a mean look.

"To answer your first question," Entice said with sass. "I'm from Queensbridge," she mentioned her neighborhood like it was self explanatory. "As for me having anything better to do, I guess not."

"I love this dame," Sparks said, tossing an arm around Entice's waist.

Markus saw her move into his body. Sparks welcomed the

embrace. Markus smiled.

"I love my clients. I'm a hand's on type manager," Sparks worded.

Markus grimaced at his words as he called the owner of Jingling Babes. They were already at the entrance of the club. Markus had a gun in his pocket. The rain was coming down. There was no turning back.

Marty, the owner of the club answered on the third ring. Markus heard the same booty shaking music within his phone emanating out of the entrance of the club. This told him Marty was inside the club.

"Hey Marty, can you hear me?" Markus asked.

"I can hear you," he yelled above all the bass in the music. "Who is this?"

"It's Markus, I'm outside."

"Markus…?" He asked, sounding confused. "I don't know a Markus."

"You know Mr. Excitement, right? Markus is Mr. Excitement. Come outside. I'm outside."

The phone connection was abruptly severed. Markus flipped his phone shut. It was raining and he wasn't sure if Marty hung up or the connection got severed. They were disconnected in any event and he wasn't going to stand outside in the rain any longer.

"I think Marty hung up on me. I ain't gonna stand in front of this club in the rain and catch the flu or pneumonia," Markus said, looking at Entice and Sparks. "Her weave looks like it's about to unravel."

"This ain't no weave," Entice snapped. "This rain is just not good for my perm."

"You two are both a bunch of bitches," Sparks worded giving both of them narrow eyes.

He was in the middle of licking a cigar. Markus laughed. He was rolling up in the middle of what was beginning to turn into a heavy shower.

"Why did he hang up on your black ass?"

"I don't know. Maybe we got disconnected."

They stood in the ever increasing rain, debating the issue. Two bouncers at the entrance frisked a couple of patrons. Marty walked out a side entrance.

"Hey Mr. Excitement," he greeted, urging them over with a wave.

He stood at the threshold of the side entrance waving. A canopy above him kept the rain off. Entice broke out in a dash toward the side door, Sparks and Markus followed suit.

Marty greeted Mr. Excitement with a hearty hug, and gave Entice and Sparks the once over. He kept his eyes locked on Entice. She was nice to look at.

"What brings you here Mr. Excitement?"

"I'm not sure yet." Markus answered with honesty.

"Oh," the club owner muttered. "I haven't seen you in half a year maybe? What have you been up to? Don't tell me, I know all about your movies and how you're making big things happen. Come inside man, it's raining cats and dogs."

"It's raining pussies and bitches," Entice said.

They all laughed and walked into the club. Marty laughed louder than anyone else. He was a jovial middle aged Jew. He led them through a corridor of many doors to the left and right. They went by doors that showed rooms full of strippers, dressing rooms. They passed by the lockers, huge mirrors, and half naked women standing. Some were bent over, stretching. Others sat on top of tables and chairs with legs crossed, or sprawling, legs wide opened, showing camel toe and clitoris piercings. Some of the dancers were wearing things on that were as thin as dental floss. Others accessorized to tantalize a man's fetish preference, nursing uniforms, Swedish maid attire, Dominatrix and leather outfits.

Sparks stopped and looked into one particular room where two strippers were getting dressed. He stared, licking his lips. They were two hot looking pieces of flesh. They saw him, and smiled. Entice grabbed him roughly by an ear, dragging him along.

"Hey, you never know. Those hos might be looking for management," Sparks worded sheepishly.

"They look like they're looking for pimps. Come on," Entice sassed.

Once they were inside Marty's office, Sparks finished rolling his blunt. While Markus, Sparks and Entice puffed and passed the smoldering weed, Marty told them about his dilemma.

"This guy Cali has completely taken over my operation. You know I try to run a respectable place here. No trouble, no police, and definitely no prostitution. Now every day the police show up. They made a full raid two weeks ago. I've never been raided before. I got a couple of police officers coming in sometimes. One wants to close me down for good, the other shakes me down for cash and take liberties with the girls. Cali has a lot of them giving blow jobs and fucking in the VIP. My whole business has turned into a whorehouse. And I just don't know what to do."

"Did you tell the cops?" Markus asked.

He heard Sparks's moan but he didn't look at him or say anything. He waited for Marty's answer.

"I want to tell the police, but I'm scared to go to them. Sometimes you can't tell a cop from a criminal. It seems like everyone is down with it. Cali is a terrible man. I'm just an old Jew who owns a strip joint. At first I had to deal with the Italians, but I was young then that's over and done with. The mob wasn't as much trouble. Cali is different. He roughs me up and he's always with three or four mean looking guys. One of them pulled a gun out on me. He was trying to force one of the girls to do things. I said something to him and he smacked me with the gun. She left and never came back. She was one of my best girls. Excitement, Tanisha's here and she's running right along with him. I think Cali is her pimp. I think all the girls are under him now."

"It seems like Cali is straight pimpin' the entire Jingling Babes," Entice told no one in particular.

"I came here to talk to Cali. It seems like we're both not happy with him," Markus said to Marty.

While Markus was talking he felt Sparks going inside his jacket pocket. He took the pistol out. Marty saw the gun.

"No, no, no…" He whined, "I don't want anymore trouble in here. I don't want any problems."

"You already gotta ass load of problems," Sparks snapped. He coughed then passed the blunt to Entice. "Consider us your problem solvers. Just stay back here where it's safe. Where is Cali?"

"He's usually in the observation room," Marty told Sparks.

"Observation room, what the fuck is that?" Sparks asked.

"A small room with a trick mirror where you can see what goes on in the main VIP lounge. Sometimes he has a video camera. He films. He told me he was making a documentary or something."

Entice barked out a laugh. "More like a porno."

"Cali is a very enterprising fella. Let's see if he can sell a

DVD of me pistol whipping his black ass," Sparks snapped. He turned to Markus. "Let's case the place then go to this observation room and have our little talk with him."

"I don't know," Markus said with uncertainty.

"What is there to know? Besides, this guy said Cali is pimpin' Tanisha. Don't you wanna save her Captain?"

"I ain't Captain save a Ho," Markus snapped at Sparks.

"Maybe not, but you've been fucking with a ho... You told me you care about her," Sparks reminded Markus.

"You're right. I do care. I guess this is more than slashed tires and broken windows."

He watched Sparks put the gun behind him in the crook of his jeans and spine. His T-shirt went down, concealing the automatic weapon. It was compact and fully loaded.

"Marty," Entice called him to her attention. "You said he has three or four dudes with him. Where are they?"

"With him in the observation room or roaming around the club, sometimes they are in here, in my office harassing me," Marty told Entice.

Suddenly they heard the door knob turning.

Although the music in the club was booming at a high volume, they could hear the door being opened. Markus figured the office was sound proofed. A goon walked inside the office.

"Haven't you heard of knocking?" Sparks growled with the blunt dangling from the side of his mouth.

Markus recognized the hoodlum. He was a guy he had seen hanging with Cali a few times. He smoked weed with him on the corner in the hood. His name was Wayne. He walked inside the office then closed the door. He was completely inside when he saw the other people in the room.

He was about to open his mouth, but Wayne's eyes widened when he saw Sparks and Markus. He knew who they were and was shocked to find them in Marty's office. Markus was as still as a mannequin. He didn't know what to do. Sparks whipped a hand behind his back, and pulled out the gun. And just like Entice warned, it was all about to go down.

The guy moved a hand toward the door. Sparks grabbed him before the door got halfway open. The booty shaking music thumped into Marty's office then got muffled when he closed the door shut.

"Where are you going nigga…?"

The gun was in Wayne's face. Markus watched as Sparks escorted Wayne to Marty's desk.

"Get your Jew ass up," Sparks snapped and Marty hopped out of the seat behind the desk. "Sit down," he ordered. Wayne sat. "You got some duct tape or something?" Sparks asked.

Before Marty could answer Wayne looked at him and said, "What the fucks going on?"

"What do you think is going on?" Sparks barked.

The gun was kissing his forehead. Wayne was trembling and Entice seemed to be enjoying it. Markus didn't think it would come down to putting guns in anyone's face. It had come down to exactly that.

"You are now officially a hostage," Sparks told Wayne with an evil grin.

"Hostage…?" Markus and Marty chorused.

"That's right," Sparks responded. "If we let him go, he'll run and tell Cali." He directed his attention toward the hostage. "Was your black ass down with the tire slashing and breaking the windows?"

"I don't know anything about nothing…" Wayne worded.

His words were punctuated by a slap across the face with the pistol.

"Yes!" Wayne said faster than Sparks could smack him with the gun again.

Sparks gave Markus a grin, "We got a confession already. See how easy things are going."

"Where is Cali?" Markus asked Wayne. He thought about things. "Where is Tanisha?"

"Somewhere on the earth," Wayne muttered.

"Somewhere on earth, huh," Sparks chuckled. "Your ass is very funny."

Marty had the duct tape somewhere in the office. While they were interrogating the hostage, the old Jew scrounged it up.

"Ah here's the tape," he uttered, nodding.

Sparks tore off a good deal of tape and wrapped it around Wayne's mouth. He looked at Markus.

"We don't need any information from his dude. All we need do is walk around and search for Cali." He directed his eyes back to Wayne. "I'm gonna wrap so much tape around your black ass and this chair, you won't be able to move your dick if that shit gets hard. I'm not even worried about you." He turned back to Markus. "I saw this shit in a movie. Sometimes the best plan is no plan at all. Tonight we're keeping it gangsta."

Markus knew what Sparks said was supposed to reassure him. But it only had the opposite effect.

Markus and Sparks left the office. They walked further into the strip club, Jingling Babes. Sparks wasn't sure about Marty. He figured once they left the office he would loosen all the tape they wrapped around Wayne. He instructed Entice to stay in the office with them. She grinned and pulled out a decent size pocket knife.

Markus decided to follow Sparks and play things by ear. He was glad Sparks took the gun from his pocket. Markus was a tall, athletically built man who didn't look like he needed a weapon to defend himself anyway.

Whirlwind, by Black Moon was thumping throughout the building. The beat was hypnotic and exotic, the perfect sort of music for a strip club. Sparks, a hip-hop connoisseur, sang along with the lyrics while they walked.

...Buck, flow with the speed of a bob sled/bust lead to the head/plus I stay red/every time I think about the dead/I think about what Machiavelli said, fight for the ones who bled/in this emcee shit, we agree shit got out of hand/but they ain't stop the plan/un-effective, no respect for this/but my perspective is/those who walk the path of the straight n narrow/we can rule the land like Pharaoh/plus enjoy the bone to the marrow/delicious, eat an emcee for breakfast to break fast/shatter niggas dreams like glass I ask/how many niggas wanna get with this shit...

The club was packed to capacity. Markus had never seen as many dudes in the joint as he had this night. Perhaps it was because of the extracurricular activities Cali had established. It was way too crowded. To distinguish one person from the next, one had to get real close.

Markus let that be known to Sparks. Sparks shrugged off his worries.

"We ain't looking for more of Cali's cronies. Marty said the VIP is on the other side of the club. That's where our black ass's is headed."

The music was way too loud and the place wasn't brightly lit, but that's where they went. The lit stage was where strippers seductively spun their gyrating bodies around poles. Half drunken men tossed bills, and put dollars in G-strings and cleavage exposed before them.

Sparks took a quick glance at the stage, and kept moving toward the other side of the club. Markus gave the stage a more thorough look because he was trying to see if Tanisha was on there. About eight dancers were on the stage. Tanisha was not one of them.

They had to brush past and bump into people as they pushed themselves through the club's patrons. No one gave them more than a half look. The men had their eyes glued to one of the dancers, or had a stripper on their lap.

Markus and Sparks walked through a draped entrance that led to a small corridor with four doors. Sparks cracked a door open and stuck his head inside. It was a cubicle that had a plush circular couch in the middle of it with a multi colored strobe light above. Two females and a dude were inside.

There was a Latin woman wearing a flimsy dress, straddling the guy and bouncing up and down. The john was moaning. Sparks knew what was going down. The other woman was on her knees on the floor. Sparks couldn't see her head because it was stuck up the other females dress. He figured she was eating the girl's ass out.

"Interesting," he mumbled, before closing the door.

"What?" Markus asked.

"Nothing, I don't think Tanisha's in there, though she could be. But if she is, her head is between some Puerto Rican's ass cheeks" Sparks laughed.

Markus pushed him aside. He was going in the room to see if Tanisha's head was inside a Puerto Rican's ass or not. Sparks grabbed his shoulder before he could open the door.

"Over here," Sparks said, pointing. One of the doors was different from the others. It appeared not all of the rooms on this side of the club were cubicles. "That must be the observation room," Sparks said, pulling out the gun. "We got two choices. We can search the rest of these cubicles, or we can go straight in there on some *Dirty Harry* shit and get this over with."

Markus began thinking about his whole life, taking everything into perspective. All that had happened in the past couple of weeks flashed through his mind. Markus knew what was beyond the door. He wasn't ready to get physical with Cali, and he wasn't ready for the emotions that would come with seeing Tanisha in a whorish situation. Markus and Tanisha were introduced directly before they fucked on film. She hadn't changed, and was only pretending. Markus was still doing porn. He didn't know why he was feeling this way toward Tanisha. He wasn't supposed to care, was he?

Markus found himself feeling more anger over the fact that Cali might possibly be pimping Tanisha than about what was done to his car. He shook his buzzing thoughts away, and got a better look at Sparks in the dimly lit area.

Sparks's eyes were gleaming with anticipation. He seemed to be enjoying things a bit too much. He was a drug dealer. Markus figured all of the gun flashing, and wrapping people with duct tape was normal to him. He realized he didn't know Sparks, really didn't know Tanisha, never wanted to know Cali, and worst of all didn't know himself.

"What is your real name?" Markus asked.

"What was that?" Sparks said. He pulled the clip out of the pistol and snapped it back in. The sound caused Markus to flinch.

"Your name…?" Markus asked. "Listen, we are about to walk through that door and possibly hurt Cali or worse and get arrested afterwards. I know we ain't gonna just scare him. I see it all in your eyes." He paused but Sparks didn't say anything. He was all ears. "Once we walk through the door I ain't gonna be talking. You can do all the talking. I'm gonna punch the nigga in his face and keep hitting him till my knuckles break. I don't feel too good. I feel light headed. Now wouldn't be a good time for me to blackout."

"Nah, it wouldn't," Sparks told him, thinking. "Nigga don't faint on me. I'll shoot Cali and leave you on the fucking floor with the smoking gun."

Markus wasn't sure if he would do that or not.

"Cory..." Sparks said his birth name with a grin.

"Cory...?" Markus broke out in a hearty laugh. "That's your fucking name?"

"Fuck you! You don't even know who you are. Your name might not be Markus. It could be Mortimer or Oliver for all you know."

"True," Markus whispered. "If I'm lucky I'll find out more about myself on Wednesday."

"Wonderful," Sparks began moving toward the door. "Now, Mortimer, would you do the honors of opening this fucking door."

"What if it's locked?" Markus asked.

"If it's locked, we'll just shoot the fucking lock off. Ain't no stopping us now..."

Markus felt like he was about to fall unconscious. He reached for the doorknob with a shaky hand. He was determined not to fail Sparks, not to fail Tanisha, and for once, not fail himself.

Nancy Adler had many things on her mind as she unclothed herself. She slowly submerged her body inside the tub. The water was hot and soothing. She needed something to ease her body and mind. All the things Gary Zimmerman said while taking her home were so strange. She couldn't stop thinking about them.

Markus Johnson was definitely the most interesting client she ever had. Gary told her about children who had their pasts completely erased. He spoke of a magician who could control and manipulate swarms of flies. He talked about the things he suspected. About how all the special children in the long ago abandoned case were all sexually molested.

He suspected some sort of huge, twisted group of individuals who kidnapped children, sold them to pedophiles, had them doing child porn and other things despicable. Nancy thought the whole thing was way beyond her. She had looked at Zimmerman in open mouth surprise and listened while he drove and spoke. She tried to determine whether he was mentally stable or not. He was talking about dark magic, about how this illusionist Randleman, the one they called Lord of the Flies, about how his magic was real. Markus Johnson was indeed a weird case.

Cali sat in a chair, leaning forward. He had an eye in a digital video camera in front of him. The video camera was on a tripod. A trick mirror showed one of the VIP room's the camera was focused on. The music was booming inside the club. He didn't notice Sparks and Markus's arrival. Someone else was in the room with Cali.

Markus directed his wavering vision away from Sparks to Cali. He felt himself within the early stages of being yanked into the blackness, the void of unconsciousness. He was so used to the sensation. He knew he had a few seconds before he was thrown into La-La-Land.

He heard commotion going on around him. It was Sparks and the other dude. He didn't divert his eyes from Cali. Cali had turned his head around, his eyes widened. Markus told Sparks he wasn't going to say anything. He didn't. He jumped on Cali in a flash of aggression and silent rage. His nemesis was a tall, slender dude. Markus was taller, more muscular. The odds were in his favor, he figured.

Cali was shocked but only for a second. Markus didn't waste any time throwing one punch after another. He wasn't sure what sort of damage he was doing. Eventually his fists started connecting with Cali's face.

Cali grunted, trying to throw a couple of punches of his own, but Markus's adrenalin was on overdrive. He didn't feel any of them. Markus kept throwing his own fists and didn't bother to block. Cali was weak. Markus felt no more than a sting when he punched his jaw. Markus threw a punch at his jaw in kind but the punch landed on his nose instead, blood flew out of a nostril. He went flying. His body knocked the camera off the tripod, his back hit the trick mirror before the rest of him slid to the ground.

"Wait!" Cali begged.

Markus was almost completely out of it. He began seeing images, the man and woman again and the little girl.

"No-o-o," he yelled.

He had to concentrate on staying conscious. He couldn't blackout now. He focused on his opponent's body up against the wall. He began kicking and stomping him, aiming his boots at Cali's face. Cali had his arms up, trying to protect his face. "You mother-fucking pussy! Why were you fucking with me? What the fuck did I ever do to you?" Markus yelled.

Cali didn't bother to answer. Markus kept stomping and kicking.

The old man with the scar emerged in front of Markus, the man grinned something evil with his lips curled... The man's mouth opened inhumanly wide, exposing a set of black teeth... Flies, thousands and millions of them flew out his mouth and gushed out at Markus in a swarm. Markus yelled something inhuman...

He jumped back, began swinging his arms wildly trying to get the flies away. They kept coming. They kept swarming around him and kept coming out of the man's mouth.

Markus knew nothing else.

Markus gained consciousness. The room was once again before him. There was no evil white man with a scar. There were no flies. He saw Sparks sitting on a chair. Cali was on the ground, he was conscious and huddled in a corner. Sparks had the gun aimed at Cali. He dared not rise. Markus tried to gather himself. He looked around. The other dude was laid out on the floor. Sparks had pistol whipped him soundly. The guy didn't look like he would cause a problem for them.

"Look," Sparks said. "Look through the trick mirror."

Markus looked. When he saw he turned away, "Shit" he uttered.

Tanisha was in the room and two men were fucking her. One had her from behind, and she had the other man's dick in her mouth. Apparently Cali was filming the situation before they rushed into the room and began dishing out violence.

"She's nothing but a ho Markus. Your ass knew what she was the day you met her. Forget about that bitch!" Sparks said, stifling a laugh.

Markus looked for a couple of seconds then he turned away. He seemed confused, dazed from the episode.

"I was out for—"

"For about five minutes. I didn't wanna stay here that long but I wasn't gonna leave you here, like that. Let's get our black asses the fuck out of here and call it a night," Sparks worded in urgency.

"Thanks," Markus said.

Sparks said, "Don't mention it."

"We gotta get out of here."

"Didn't I just say that? You beat the shit out of Cali. He's either gonna try to kill you or he's gonna be so scared he's gonna leave you alone. It's one or the other. I'm proud of your black ass. I feel like crying. Damn! I didn't think you'd bring it like that."

"Neither did I, Sparks, I need to get Tanisha out of here."

"Why?" He questioned. "I bet you she's enjoying it. Take a look at her do what she does. I see why you were always going over to her crib. That bitch can suck and…"

"Alright Sparks!" Markus snapped.

"It ain't easy being Captain Save-a-Ho, is it? What is your ass gonna do? Rush in there, pull those niggas off of her, pick her ho ass up, and go running off into the sunset with that bitch over your shoulders."

Sparks spoke then walked over to Cali. He whacked him across the jaw with the pistol. Markus was pretty sure Cali was knocked out now. Sparks reach into a pocket and pulled out the roll of duct tape.

"We gotta wrap these jerks up. Cali's gonna wanna kill us. Fuck him being scared, I think this is gonna turn into war. I suggest you move."

Markus said, "Move, I don't know what you mean? Like us leaving the club?"

"No jerk. I mean move like from where you live."

"Move, where?" Markus asked.

An up and coming porn star, he had a little cash stashed away, emphasis on a little. He understood what Sparks meant. He just wasn't sure how he was going to get it done.

"Move anywhere. Sign that contract and give it to the dude who owns Smut Central. Get that money. Get your black ass a house in Jersey, up in the hills like rappers do. Give me a hand."

He gave Sparks a helping hand. They found another chair and put both chairs beside each other. They put an unconscious Cali and his companion on the chairs, sitting them upright. Sparks wrapped so much duct tape around them, they looked like mummies. Cali had gained back consciousness during but he was way too weak to put up a fight. Once he started throwing death threats Markus grabbed the tape from Sparks and wrapped some around his mouth. He didn't want to hear anything Cali had to say.

"Let's go save that ho, Captain," Sparks snickered to Markus.

"I feel like I'm gonna blackout again," Markus told him. "Let's get Entice and go. I wanna go home."

"No way, your black ass can't go home, remember. You gotta move. The hood's no longer safe for you anymore. Cali may seem like a pussy now, but as soon as he gets out of all of that tape. He's gonna be like Suge Knight."

Markus thought about something, "What about Marty?"

Sparks thought about that, "Fuck him. His Jew ass will weasel his way out of shit. You gotta worry about yourself. That and you gotta worry about how much shit Tanisha knows and is gonna tell Cali."

"Tanisha isn't gonna tell Cali anything, I'm sure of that," Markus snapped to her defense.

Once upon a time Tanisha doing anything to harm him would have seemed impossible. Now he wasn't sure of anything. Cali knew about Gwyneth and Emily's whereabouts. That was something he continued to ponder the moment he left Gwyneth's building and saw his car was vandalized again.

Sparks nudged his jaw at the trick mirror. "Look, look at her looking at the mirror. She's looking where she thinks the camera is. Who knows what she told him."

Markus didn't say anything. He didn't know what he would

do once he was in the room. There were so many things he didn't know.

Sparks and Markus went back to Marty's office. Ironically, Sparks told Marty to call the cops.

"Call the police as soon as we're ghost."

"That means we're leaving…" Entice said to Marty, happy to see Markus and Sparks.

She gave them both a kiss, and put her pocket knife away. "He was gonna unravel the tape. I let him know that wouldn't be such a good idea, so he chilled," Entice said, looking at Marty with scrutiny.

"Sorry," Marty blurted.

"So am I. I'm sorry for bringing you more trouble," Markus told him.

Sparks said "More trouble…? Are you kidding me, Markus? We probably helped more than the both of you think. Cali won't be fucking around this place no more, once the police arrive. Knowing him, he'll be way too busy trying to kill us. He won't have time for filming porn or pimpin. Let's go,"

Markus, Entice and Sparks marched out the strip club, heading to Sparks's parked car.

23

Markus had additional things to worry about besides his lost past. His present was now something for him to worry about. He sat in the back of Sparks's car not knowing where they were going and not caring. Markus figured Sparks would have to evacuate the hood as well. He questioned Sparks about his situation. When he answered Markus was shocked.

"I don't live in that hood," Sparks told him.

"I thought…" Markus uttered before Sparks cut him off.

"You thought your hood was my hood. Never shit where you eat. I sell drugs there, but I live somewhere else," Sparks worded, turning his head to the backseat with a wide grin. "Now your black ass knows why you chose me as your manager."

Markus grimaced. He didn't choose him for anything. There was always someone steering Markus in one direction or another. He was used to being steered. He thought about Tanisha. He was tired of directing her life the way people like Gwyneth and her husband did for him. Driving Tanisha had come to an end. Markus figured it was Sparks's turn behind the wheel of his life.

He began thinking about Michelle while they drove. Her lovely image went strolling through his mind. The same way it did when he was about to open the observation room door at Jingling Babes, and while he was beating on Cali. He caught a glimpse of Michelle during those two instances, just for a passing beat. The image of her was now imprinted all over his brain. Thinking about her with such intensity, was enough to cause a blackout.

Markus awoke a couple minutes after twelve noon on Tuesday. A splitting headache prevented him from concentrating too hard. He didn't know where he was. Rising from the couch, Markus looked around. The place looked like the inside of someone's living room. He figured the place belonged to Sparks, but wasn't sure who carried him here. Markus tried real hard to think.

He remembered being in Sparks's car and blacking out. The shock of cold water splashing his face brought him out of his trance. He opened his eyes and there was the soft face of Entice. She roused him from La-La-Land by dousing him with water from a bottle.

His memory jogged back to getting out of the car. Sparks asked him for his house keys. Markus had asked why.

"I'm gonna get a few of my peoples to go to your crib and get a few things. It's best if you don't show your black ass for fucking forever."

He remembered saying thanks, reaching down into his jeans pocket, and handing him the keys. He walked in building and into Sparks's apartment. Markus immediately flopped on a couch and fell into a deep slumber.

Now wide awake with a splitting headache, Markus wondered where Sparks had gone.

"Sparks, Entice…?" He shouted. "Is anyone here?"

"You're back amongst the living."

It was the voice of Entice. She was in another room. Markus became less anxious and reclined on the couch.

"I need some aspirins," he shouted.

"I don't know what's in this apartment," she answered.

"How about looking through the medicine cabinet or something?"

"I'll check but he doesn't even have food in the fridge. I think the only drugs you'll find in here are the illegal sort."

"Where did Sparks go?"

"He went to see about your stuff. He went to look for your contracts and legal stuff and for the rest of your identification," Entice said, floating into the living room.

"Hi…" he said, getting up and walking by her as she was approaching him.

"Do you want me to go to the store?" She asked.

"Yeah, get me some Tylenol or something and get us some food."

"Ok," she said.

Markus felt her eyes watching him until he shut the bathroom door. He turned on the sink's faucet and splashed cold water on his face. The need to thank Sparks for thinking so fast grew, but he also wanted to punch him in the face for what he got him into.

When they were inside Jingling Babes, he did want to get back at Cali. He couldn't think of any other way to respond to Cali's antics. It was easy for Sparks to convince him to respond with violence. Markus was so accustomed to other people dictating his existence. All Sparks had to do was grab the reins. Shacking up with Sparks was out of the question. He definitely had to find another place to live. He didn't want to be around anyone right now. Wednesday would come and he hoped Gary Zimmerman was as good a hypnotist as he was at pretending to be an alcoholic.

He was more excited about seeing Nancy than the possibility of his hidden memories returning. He dared not think about Michelle but not thinking about her seemed impossible. The room began spinning with his thoughts. He felt the same lightheadedness like he was about to blackout again. Markus wasn't sure how long he was struggling to remain conscious, but Entice was back from the store.

"Are you alright?" He heard her ask with concern.

"No," he answered. "You got those aspirins."

Entice handed him a bottle of Tylenol. She went in the kitchen to get a glass of water. He didn't wait for her return. Markus gobbled up three capsules. When she came back into the living room with the water he took the glass. Without drinking it, he placed the glass on the floor. Markus reached up and pulled Entice on the couch.

"I need something to keep my mind off her," he said.

Markus saw the confused look Entice wore. She wasn't sure if he was referring to Tanisha or Michelle. He was thinking of sucking her nipples, concentrating on her breasts when all of sudden, everything became blurry. He reached for her but it seemed as if his arms were midget's arms, as much as he stretched them, his hands couldn't reach Entice.

Markus felt like he was drunk. The expanse of the living

room beyond the couch and her nice shape was an unrecognizable haze. His eyes monopolized on Entice. If he would have looked anywhere else he would have fainted. With dizziness he eventually connected with Entice. He unbuttoned the first two on her shirt, till her boobs showed. He began massaging her breasts. He shook his head trying desperately to stop the room from spinning, and unbuttoned two more buttons. Entice had a confused smile, looking into his eyes. She helped unbutton the rest.

"When did Sparks say he was gonna get back?" He asked while they took off her shirt.

"He didn't," she answered.

Her breath was sweet. Entice stood long enough to kick off her sneakers, and slipped out her jeans. Her legs were slightly parted. The gap that shaped her slender hips was wide in the middle. She was sexy. Markus was immediately aroused.

"He didn't say much. We are all the way up in the Bronx. I don't think he'll be back anytime soon." She thought about things then said. "What does it matter if he comes back anytime soon or not?"

Markus was way too confused and dizzy to think and distinguish one thing from the next. If he thought too much he would think about Michelle. Then he would be back in La-La-Land.

Entice started helping Markus take off his clothes. He moved his face toward a breast and began sucking her nipple. Her nipples perked pointy. She was just as aroused as he. Entice wanted him. She had delicate fingers and long nails. Her hands were feeling good as she raked his back with perfectly manicured talons. She used them while she took off what he was wearing. He continued sucking alternately from one nipple to the next. Once he was completely naked she grabbed his face and directed his attention to her eyes.

Markus didn't pay much attention to Entice the first time he met her. Minutes after being introduced, they were in a hotel suite, fucking with Daisy Lace calling the shots. Markus felt Entice pushing him back. She opened her legs wider.

"I know you're hungry. C'mon and eat."

Hungry or not, he wasn't sure, but he knew he was fading out. He kept his mental focused on Entice, kept thinking about anything but Michelle. He could barely see the woman who was directing his head between her legs. He allowed her to guide him down. He was helplessly sedated.

First he began blacking out then he began seeing things before he blacked out, now he had crazy dreams and slept for unusual lengths of time. He would see the flies and the man with the scar on his face. Markus not only saw this man, he was beginning to feel fearful of him. He had to get his mind off of things before things got worse. Sex in some shape, form or fashion always seemed to be the remedy for him. He figured what was between Entice's legs would cure his immediate situation.

Entice's beauty wasn't overly obvious like Michelle's. Michelle's appearance was wondrous. She was lighter skinned than Entice, more his complexion. She was slender and outstandingly proportioned to perfection.

Michelle was a man's dream, a woman who looked like she could be a movie star, or a super model. He didn't know who Michelle was or what she did. All he knew was that he was staring at Entice but seeing Michelle.

Entice was the sort of girl you saw in a rap music video. He was quite sure she was a video vixen before she wound up being introduced to Tony "Tee-Neck" Jersey. Now she served as a distraction to keep him from blacking out. He refused to allow it to happen without a

Entice didn't blame Markus for falling unconscious between her legs. She moved his head and put him in a comfortable position on the couch. She slipped back into her jeans and put her shirt on. After that she went into the bedroom.

A couple of hours later, Sparks came back carrying the things he took from Markus's place. Entice greeted him with a hug and kiss. Sparks patted her on the ass then looked over at Markus.

"Is he sleeping or did he blackout again?" He asked.

"What's the difference?" She replied.

Sparks nodded his head. All that mattered was he retrieved Markus's important papers. He was able to retrieve the contracts and a few other useful things. He saw exactly how much Smut Central Entertainment offered Markus. It was more than enough. All they had to do was find a good realtor somewhere in Jersey or Connecticut.

Sparks was making plans for Markus and his money.

He got a better look at Entice and grinned. In a pair of his boxers and one of his tee-shirts on, she was looking good. He knew she was watching television in the bedroom before he walked in.

"You sleeping on the couch with Mr. Excitement or are you coming in the bedroom with me?" He asked.

"Where do you want me?" She replied.

He showed her where he wanted her. He motioned a hand. She obediently moved closer. They embraced.

"Mr. Excitement doesn't seem very exciting tonight."

He grabbed her hands and moved them to his crotch. He was fully erect. "I'm very excited."

"I guess you'll have to do then," she laughed.

"I guess my black ass will," he said with a frown.

He guided her into the bedroom, flung her on the bed. Entice started undressing and Sparks did the same. He wasn't sure what she was all about, but he knew she was sexy and more than willing to fuck on command. She was so good looking. He instantly went between her legs to eat her pussy. Sparks was horny but above and beyond that he was focused.

He was focused on Markus's future and his. He figured Entice would wear him out and he would get a good night sleep. Once the morning presented itself he would take Markus to the Smut Central office with those contracts signed. Then they would use the upfront money specified in the contract to put a down payment on some sort of house or condo, a residence far away from the hood, Cali and all the bullshit.

When Sparks went to Brooklyn earlier he saw a few dudes he knew were friends of Cali. It was all he could do to avoid them. He felt like a sucker sneaking around, but all he needed to do was get the important stuff and bounce. He had the plane tickets Tee-Neck gave Markus and the script Daisy Lace wrote.

Sparks didn't wait for Entice to decide if she wanted to sign with Smut Central, he decided for her. The flight to Japan wouldn't include her but the movie script had a part that had Entice's name written all over it. That triple X movie wouldn't start filming until they got back from the job in the Orient. Vonchell was scheduled to take the Japan trip. Markus had two plane tickets. Sparks already made the other ticket his. He wasn't sure if Vonchell had a manager but he was going to find out in Japan. Sparks saw so many possibilities and endless money. He liked the managerial situation.

He thoroughly licked, slobbered, and plunged his tongue in and out of Entice's hot pussy. Sparks flipped her over on her stomach. Her butt was like a gift from Mother Nature. He watched the thing of wonder for a minute then commanded her to spread her butt cheeks wider. Eagerly she obliged giggling. Taking her from the rear was going to be such a wonderful experience, Sparks licked his lips. He already foamed her pussy up with saliva. She was glistening from her inner thigh region. Entice was dripping with moisture. His pulsating dick throbbed with anticipation.

Markus was roused out the darkness of sleep by a very energetic Sparks.

"Get up nigga," Sparks worded. "We got a meeting with Tee-Neck bright and early, and it's already bright and early."

Markus shook his shoulders. "What day is it?" He asked, sounding confused.

It was Wednesday morning and Markus was still half sleep.

He had been having a terrible dream, but could barely remember it. All he knew was the dream consisted of flies, hundreds and thousands of them. And there was the man with the wicked scar across his face. Markus shivered thinking about him.

Inside the bathroom, Entice laid out some clothes for him to wear. Markus grimaced. They were clothes retrieved from his apartment. He wondered what else was salvaged but he was way too dazed to dwell on anything besides hygiene.

Markus took a long shower, flossed and brushed his teeth. He was surprised Sparks had dental floss handy, but then he gave the box a second look, and realized it was something he took from his apartment. It made him laugh.

"Did you take my toilet paper off the spool as well?" He yelled out the bathroom door.

Sparks didn't answer. Once Markus got himself together they left the apartment, hopped inside Sparks's car and drove to Smut Central Entertainment.

Tony Jersey, affectionately known as Tee-Neck was sitting at his desk, puffing on a fat Cuban cigar. He just gave the secretary the okay to let Markus, Sparks and Entice in, but Sparks was halfway inside the office before she gave them permission to enter.

"Tony," Sparks uttered like he knew Tony Jersey for half of his life. "How about one of those cigars, goomba…?"

"How about, who the hell are you?" Tee-Neck barked, rising off his chair.

His eyes narrowed Chinese-like until Entice walked into the door, Markus followed. "Who is this character?" The balding Italian asked with irritation.

"This character is Mr. Excitement and Entice's new management," Sparks answered with a smile.

With a freshly rolled blunt in one hand, Sparks walked closer to Tee-Neck's desk, and grabbed the Zippo lighter.

"Excitement signed the contract. I find them reasonable though moneywise, Entice's contract is a bit thin."

Tee-Neck laughed. "Whaddya talking about…? She's new in the business," he winked at her. "The contract is only for a year. If things go well we renegotiate," The balding Italian said grabbing the Zippo from Sparks before he was able to flick it. "Nothing comes off my desk unless I want it. You got that?"

Sparks's eyes widened before he laughed. "I got it."

"Good."

"Here is my contract all signed Mr. Jersey," Entice said with a small voice.

She was wearing something very simple, a sun dress with sandals. It was a very hot day. Tee-Neck gave her the once over, grabbed the papers, looked for the signature and smiled.

Sparks gave Tee-Neck Markus's papers. Tee-Neck looked for the signature.

"Good for you boy," he said. "I'm gonna cut you two your signing bonus."

"I would appreciate it," Markus told Tee-Neck. "I gotta find myself a new place to live."

"Is that so?" Tee-Neck asked, sitting down. "I might be able to help you. I own a good bit of real-estate."

"Do you, where?" Sparks inquired.

"Where ever I want." Tee-Neck coughed out some cigar smoke. "Don't ever question me."

Sparks was going to ask him another question but Markus placed a finger up to his lips. Sparks managed to remain silent for as long as it took Tee-Neck to write out two checks. Tee-Neck reminded Markus about Japan, it was two weeks away. Markus had a passport somewhere. He hoped Sparks retrieved it from the apartment. He told Tee-Neck he was ready for the trip to the orient.

Entice inquired about the trip, but Sparks told her not to worry. He asked Tee-Neck if he had another one of those scripts handy. At first he didn't know what Sparks was talking about. Then his eyes showed recognition. The new movie Daisy Lace wrote. Tee-Neck didn't know whether to ignore Sparks or swat him away like a fly. He eventually, after a long leer reached into one of his desk drawers, and pulled out a copy of the script.

"I think Entice would be perfect for the Amanda part," Sparks suggested while handing the script to Entice.

"We will see what Daisy Lace says," Tee-Neck said, winking at Entice. "Get the fuck out of my office!" he barked with aggression.

Sparks watched Markus and Entice walk out the door. He looked at the blunt he was holding and took a deep breath. The Zippo lighter was back on the desk. He looked at his nicely rolled blunt again. He took a step toward the desk, reached for the lighter.

"Do you know what get the fuck out means?" Tee-Neck barked.

"I sure do. Listen Tony," Sparks began.

"That's Tee-Neck. A guy like you better call me Tee-Neck."

"Of course, pardon me. You mentioned real-estate. Markus really needs a place to live. He has a bit of a problem where he is now."

"What sort of a problem?" He asked.

"Not the sort he needs you for, if I figured you out correctly."

He saw Tee-Neck smirk. "But he does need a place to go, like yesterday."

"I got this place in Jersey, a huge house where we film sometimes during the spring and summer when Daisy wants to shoot scenes outside. I haven't used the place in years. I can rent it out to Markus real cheap."

"We might have to take a look at the…" Sparks started but saw Tee-Neck's frown and changed directions. "Markus will take it. How much will this cost? Where is this place located?"

"I'll take care of everything. You'll get a call tomorrow morning. A good friend of mine is gonna call, a guy named Petey. He'll take care of everything."

"That sounds great, Tony. I mean Tee-Neck. Listen," Sparks said, moving closer to the desk and placing his elbows on it. "If I got out of line earlier, I apologize."

Tee-Neck laughed. "I like your spunk, boy. But you gotta learn how to follow directions. Get your elbows off my desk."

"I'll try to be more obedient," Sparks deadpanned and slowly moved away from Tee-Neck's desk.

"See that you do. Get the fuck out."

Sparks made his exit.

Markus and Entice waited for Sparks downstairs in the lobby. He told them about the house in Jersey. Markus shrugged his shoulders. He had nothing to say. He frowned at Sparks and figured his manager would take care of things. He had other matters troubling him. "I need you to drive me somewhere," Markus said.

"Where…?"

"To Gwyneth's, I gotta see about my car."

"Fine we'll do that and then—"

"I just need you to drop me off. I'll be fine after that. I got an appointment with my shrink later, and I got a couple of other things to take care of before then," Markus said, cutting Sparks short.

"Are you gonna be okay?" Sparks asked with concern, though he seemed more concerned about the blunt he was holding.

He scrounged inside a pocket and pulled out a Zippo lighter. Markus took one look at the lighter and frowned. It looked like Tee-Neck's lighter. "Entice can hang out with you until you see your shrink."

"I don't need a babysitter."

Markus left the building and walked to where the car was parked. Sparks and Entice followed suit. Sparks looked like he wanted to say more but didn't. Markus told him to find a bank. Sparks smiled a big one. He was going to cash that big check Tee-Neck wrote him.

After Markus took care of things at the bank, he hopped inside the car, and gave Sparks an envelope. "This should cover your expenses and handle the living arrangements for a couple of months."

"Tee-Neck said someone is gonna call us tomorrow. I'm gonna drop you where you wanna go, just make sure you come back to my place tonight. I don't want anything happening to you. We got that trip to Japan in two weeks."

Markus nodded. The Japan trip was so important because it was the first movie Markus filmed with Smut Central Entertainment under contract. He had to show Tee-Neck he was worth the six digits they were paying him this year. Before then he had to make every attempt to get his life in order. He had to hold confidence in Zimmerman and hypnosis. He had to have faith in Nancy fixing his brain up afterwards.

Markus was quite certain the weird dreams had something to do with this past he couldn't seem to remember. The session tonight was going to change his life forever, he was sure of it. Gary said he could rid the blackouts with hypnotism. That would be enough to make Markus content.

Even if the blackouts were curable there were still the flashbacks, the mysterious, beautiful Michelle, the man and woman who might possibly be his parents. There was a crying little girl, and that evil looking man with the wicked scar on his face. Flies everywhere and everything Markus Johnson thought about became infested with them.

25

Tuesday night at 11:36 p.m. Jonathan Manners was pronounced dead. Valencia, the maid, had given Markus the news as he walked in the penthouse apartment. Emily came running out of nowhere and jumped into her father's arms. He didn't even get a chance to think about things.

"How's my little girl?" He asked kissing and hugging her.

He held his daughter for what seemed like forever. Emily was the only concrete thing in his existence. He wanted to hold onto her forever. Markus reluctantly put her down. He went to one knee to address her at eye level. "How are you?"

"I'm good. I'm going shopping today with mommy," she said happily. "Mommy said that I can get whatever I like. I want a pony."

Markus smiled as wide as he could. He was certain Emily didn't know of Jonathan Manners demise. She wouldn't have been as happy as she was if she did.

Markus knew Jonathan had some sort of salary cap on Gwyneth. It wasn't a prenuptial, but she was only allowed to use a certain amount of cash a month. She was always complaining about how it wasn't enough money for her. Now that her husband was dead she had millions. Markus had little feelings for Jonathan Manners. Jonathan had cared for Emily like she was his very own daughter. In the Manners residence, Jonathan had been the most sensible person. Markus wasn't sure what would happen now that he was deceased. Gwyneth was one crazy, unpredictable bitch.

"Where is your mother?" Markus asked.

"She's upstairs, in the gym."

"I'm gonna go say hi to mommy. Have Valencia dress you real pretty. I'm gonna take you shopping. I won't buy you a pony, but I'll get you whatever else you want."

Markus never bothered to knock when he entered a room in the Manners residence. There was no respect for anyone and knocking mattered very little. This time he wished he had.

When he walked in the gym he saw that Gwyneth wasn't alone. He should have known something was going on by the way the maid was looking at him when he entered the penthouse, but he shrugged it off. He figured her sour face was because of Jonathan's death. But Gwyneth was always up to some mischief. He wasn't too surprised by what he saw, but it disturbed him to no end. Not out of jealously, but because he knew his daughter could have walked into the gym just as easily as he.

Gwyneth was inside on a mat wearing a tennis dress and a sports bra. Her legs were split as wide as they could go. A man was stretching her legs and eating her pussy. Gwyneth wasn't overly involved because she saw Markus as he barged in. She looked up from the head between her legs to Markus's face. She gave him a devilish smile.

"Hmm... You still haven't learned how to knock," Gwyneth moaned, faking annoyance.

"Who is this?" Markus asked, looking at who was between her legs.

A young European dude, probably her personal trainer by the way he was dressed. The guy hastily turned around when he heard Markus's voice. He jumped. His mouth was glistening with Gwyneth's secretions.

"Leave," Markus said with the meanest voice and look he could muster.

The dude ran out the door. Before Gwyneth could get off the mat, Markus said, "Jonathan Manners is dead."

"Question or statement, because you say it as if I wasn't aware," she laughed. "I was at the hospital when he passed. I saw him gasp his last breath."

"You probably strangled that last breath out of him," Markus said with little humor.

"Why are you here?"

"Why was that man between your legs?"

"Between a woman's legs is where a man is supposed to be. You should know this better than anyone in the world. Do you want to continue where he left off, Mr. Excitement?"

"I'd sooner be where Jonathan is." Markus wanted to strangle the life out of her, but was more intrigued by Jonathan Manners death. "Emily could have walked in here as easily as I did."

"No she would not. She knocks because she has got better

manners than you," She snapped and continued to stretch, only this time standing.

"How did he go?" He asked.

"Respiratory problems…"

"I thought he was sick with some rare bone disease."

"He was."

"What now?"

"I don't know what you mean by that," Gwyneth said giving Markus a curious look.

"You know damn well what I mean!" He roared.

He took a step closer. He seemed ready to deal out violence. Gwyneth laughed at his appearance and anger.

"That outburst almost made me cum," she blurted with mirth.

She walked over to a table and reached for a box of Virginia Slims. There was a lighter on the table as well. He watched her smoke the cigarette. She was looking him over as she puffed. She was sweating. She looked very good for her age.

"What now?" Markus asked.

"Now I shop. Now I fire every asshole at the brokerage firm. Now I start to live my life," she laughed in a sinister tone. "Do you know how long I've waited for this? You have no a clue. And now it's finally here."

"The many times you begged me to murder Jonathan was more than enough clues," Markus said dryly. "I wasn't talking about you. I meant what now for me. What are you gonna do about Emily and me. The whole baby idea was Jonathan's idea, not yours. You didn't want it just as much as I. Every nasty little trick or scheme you two situated around me was more his, than yours. You were never that smart. But Jonathan Manners is dead, the devil is gone. Now what is gonna happen to me and my daughter?"

"Nothing is gonna happen to you and *my* daughter. Everything is going to remain the way it is now. Nothing's going to change. You're going to continue to fuck me, and I'm going to continue to allow you visitation privileges. What made you think things would change?" Gwyneth laughed in his face. "I promised you nothing. You were supposed to kill Jonathan for me years ago. I only promised you things if you did, and you didn't. You always had some excuse but the only excuse was that you were scared. Not even custody of Emily could give you the balls to do what I wound up…" she paused, changing directions. "It wound up happening on its own…"

"You asked me to kill a man like it was a simple thing, a man who provided for me, a man who educated me!"

Markus wanted to strangle the life out of her. He cared little for Jonathan but he cared even less for Gwyneth. He rushed her, grabbed her by the neck, and forcefully moved her away from the table. He backed her body against a wall. Markus's face rammed into hers so hard it nearly sent her unconscious.

He was breathing heavily, his eyes were bloodshot. Gwyneth let out a pathetic yelp.

"You're hurting me," she whined with what little air she could get out of her lungs.

Markus was so enraged that he wanted to strike Gwyneth. It excited her, but she was scared as well. He had never assaulted her with such intensity. She wasn't sure what he was going to do next.

"You're going to kill me for a man who hid the truth from you? This is a man who had you fucking his wife while he watched because he was too sick to do it himself."

"I'm gonna kill you for myself," Markus yelled. Everything Gwyneth said reached his sensibility. "What do you mean by hid the truth?" He asked.

"Markus," she wheezed, attempting to squirm out of his grasp. "You can't possibly be as dumb as you look. Do you honestly believe we simply found you out on the street, in some park?" She laughed. "Where you think we found you I would never dream of going in a nightmare."

"What?" Markus couldn't believe what she was saying. "I was out on the streets for months after I ran away from the orphanage. You guys were walking through the park and found me curled up on a bench, scared, homeless and hungry."

"Jonathan has never walked since I've known him. He purchased you for my birthday. You were a gift. I was tired of getting run through by Jonathan's friends and the male prostitutes we picked up from the street. I wanted something more stable and someone with a huge penis. I wanted something, someone I could control. You were young but genetically sound, black, and beautiful. I knew once you reached sixteen or so you would be packing something. I was right. And you loved me. I was your beautiful white thang. You made me feel like I was worth something."

He wanted to choke the life out of Gwyneth, murder her where he had her propped against the wall. He didn't want to believe anything she said, but everything she said sounded like the truth. His head began spinning like a carrousel. He saw Jonathan Manners and Gwyneth walking through Central Park. He had seen Jonathan walking. There was no wheelchair. He was using his legs. Markus became even more confused.

Flies swarmed everywhere, buzzing, whispering words he couldn't understand. All the kids in the room were crying, yelling, whining. He was in the middle of the room, in the middle of a sea of children but he saw the light seeping in through the crack under the door, he felt the air. It was fresh and not filled with the stench of sweat, feces and piss.

Markus was somewhere else, no he thought, I'm still in the room just alone. There were no flies, no children, the door was wide open. He inhaled the freshness of the air. He was ready to leave, ready to escape, finally. Then something came rolling inside the room, it was a wheelchair, Jonathan Manners' wheelchair...

Markus was in the early stages of blacking out. He was seeing glimpses of his past. Finally, he realized the truth. What he was seeing wasn't the past. What he saw before his mind shifted back to reality, shifted back to the gym and Gwyneth was Jonathan Manners' wheelchair, but his memory showed Jonathan walking. He knew which was real and which wasn't now. He knew he was blacking out.

Gwyneth knew something was wrong because the fingers wrapped around her neck loosened. She slid to the floor gasping for much needed air. Markus stumbled a few steps. He couldn't breathe.

"I see Jonathan walking, but I hear someone telling me that he can't walk," Markus told the air.

He staggered out the gym and began stumbling down the flight of stairs that lead to the main floor of the penthouse. He promised his daughter he would take her shopping but he knew Gwyneth would do it. He hoped his daughter wouldn't see him staggering and stumbling on his way out.

Valencia was busy dusting in the entrance hall. Markus almost kicked a vase over and knocked her down. She uttered something in Italian but said nothing more nor did she hinder his path. Markus turned the doorknob and crawled out the front door before he blacked out.

Nancy Adler's secretary notified her that a ragged looking Markus Johnson was in the waiting room. He was over four hours early for his appointment. Nancy was surprised.

"He just walked in the waiting room and sat down. Mr. Johnson has not said anything. What shall I do Dr. Adler?"

"Do nothing," Nancy said over the intercom. "Let him sit there." She thought things over and said, "Stephanie cancel all of my appointments for the remainder of the day. When Mr. Watson leaves allow Markus Johnson to enter."

"Are you serious?"

"Very serious," she said with uncertainty. "And you can have the rest of the day off, Stephanie."

"But—" the secretary began to speak.

"That will be all, Stephanie," Dr. Adler said more sternly than she wanted.

Nancy moved away from her desk and sat on the chair that was always adjacent to the couch. Mr. Watson was in the middle of some revelation about himself when the session was interrupted by the secretary's dilemma.

"I apologize for that interruption," Dr. Adler said to her patient. "Please continue..."

He did. He began speaking as if there was never an interruption. Dr. Adler was distracted and wasn't as diligently listening as she should have been. Markus was nearly four hours early, something must have happened. Why is he here at the office so early? She mused.

Once the session was over and the patient had left the office, Nancy went to her desk. She was going to find out what was going on momentarily. There had not been a dull moment when it came to Mr. Excitement. She was thinking about him more than she professionally should have since Monday's session. Gary wasn't expected at the office until eight p.m. Markus obviously wanted to speak with her alone and in confidence before the actual session was underway.

Markus walked into the office and sat on the couch with his head propped up by his hands. He looked drained of all energy. Nancy Adler watched him, not knowing what to do. She gathered herself and was back into psychiatrist mode.

"Why are you here so early?" she asked him.

"They didn't accidentally stumble upon me on some park bench."

"What are you talking about?" She questioned. "Who are they?"

"Jonathan and Gwyneth," he answered. "Gwyneth told me I was a gift, a birthday present. Jonathan purchased me."

"Purchased you?" She exasperated with outright shock and confusion. "I don't understand. What do you mean by purchased?"

"I don't know what she meant, but it sounded like the truth. After she told me this I began feeling lightheaded. I was blacking out again. I tried to walk away, almost made it but only got to the front door, and I was back in La-La-land. I had more flashbacks. I'm more than certain someone's played with my mind."

"What did you see this time?" Nancy probed.

"What didn't I see? I had a series of flashbacks but I don't think they're flashbacks anymore. I think they're false images or situations. I can't explain it. What does Michelle have to do with any of this? What does she have to do with Jonathan and Gwyneth, and purchasing me? Why do I remember Jonathan walking when he's never ever been without his wheelchair since I've known him?"

"I don't know." Dr. Adler was beyond confused. "You said so much and I don't understand most of it. Markus are you ok? Markus, Markus…"

There was a man with a scar on his face, standing in front of a boy sitting on a chair. The man had his stopwatch and it was spinning, moving back and forth in front of the boy's face. The people around them were just as mesmerized as the little boy was.

"This isn't what the scientists think. This is what Franz Mesmer has been telling the world all along, this is magic. This is a beautifully dark art long gone. Most only know a fraction of what I know. This is the reason why most cannot do what I do. What I am doing now is what I call reprogramming. This is a very delicate hypnotic procedure because this boy has already been hypnotized with a different identity and past and now I am going to wipe that out and implant a completely new personification."

The people listened to the man and looked at the boy as he sat on the chair. His eyes were wide open. He had been sitting that way for hours and hadn't blinked once since the man put him under hypnosis. Flies were buzzing around the boy's head, moving in a uniformed fashion that defied logic. The man with the scar began using words that none of the people had ever heard before. They were words rarely spoken by man, an ancient tongue far removed from civilization.

The people listened with eerie attention and silence till the man began speaking English again. "One particular client wants a sex slave for his wife. I am now instilling in the subject latent suggestible things that will allow him to fulfill those tasks even though the subject is young and hasn't experienced things of a sexual nature before. Behold what I call the Randleman Machine, assistant if you will."

An attractive, young lady walked into the room rolling a chair that had a crude looking machine attached to it. It looked very much like an electric chair.

"Doctor Randleman, you said he is being reprogrammed. What was he programmed for initially?" A person asked.

"Athleticism," Randleman answered. He uttered the word, "rise" and the boy stood. He said, "Sit" and the boy went over to the machine and sat.

Immediately Randleman's assistant began connecting the boy to the weird looking chair apparatus. A helmet was placed over his head. The lovely assistant activated the machine, lights began flashing and a humming noise was heard throughout the room.

"This particular specimen was designed to be a football player or something of that nature. His psyche is implanted with things that will allow him to one day be as physically fit as possible. Now this doesn't mean he will become a sports star but with the right urging and guidance he will. All the psychological aspects are now about to be imbedded in his subconscious mind with the Randleman machine, *information, notions and things that will encourage him to excel are about to be placed within his mind through audio and visual aid. We acquire our subjects when they are young, preferably 10 or younger. Sometimes they are obtained the day they were born. We acquire them from drug addicts and pregnant runaways, women who are giving their kids up for adoption. We use kids whom are less likely to be missed. Then they are purchased and placed back into the populace, and either adopted or discovered. They are rarely noticed or thought of till they are grown, grown and superstars."*

"What happened?" Markus uttered.

He saw the way Dr. Adler was looking at him. Her face was an expression of fright.

"You blacked out again," Nancy said. "You were about to tell me something. We were talking about your recent flashback. Then you started mumbling. I didn't understand and then you just fainted."

"This shit is getting worse. If you get my meaning…?"

"What triggered the blackout this time? Was I pressuring you, maybe asking you too many questions?" She inquired.

"I'm not sure. I don't know what's going on. I started thinking about Michelle again. Maybe that was what sent me to La-La-Land. How long was I unconscious?"

"I walked in at eight o'clock sharp. I would say you were out a little less than four hours," Gary Zimmerman worded.

Markus didn't realize Gary Zimmerman was in the room until he had spoken. He was sitting on a chair on the side of the couch. He gave Markus a weird smile.

"Oh…"

"Shall we begin our hypnosis session?" Gary asked.

"Do you think that's wise Gary? I mean he just woke…" Nancy spoke with concern.

"Now is fine, Nancy. I wanna get this over with," Markus said.

"I figured you would," Gary said.

"Who is Franz Mesmer and who is Randleman? What is the Randleman Machine?" Markus questioned.

Those two names made Gary arch an eyebrow. "I've never heard of anything called the Randleman Machine. But I've heard of Randleman and Mesmer. Where have you heard of them?" Gary asked.

"Where…? I guess when I blacked out the last time. I don't seem to remember much of what I saw the last time I went unconscious. I remember flies, and a time piece spinning in front of my face, and I remember those two names."

"Interesting…" Gary mused.

"Markus has been telling me some very strange and interesting things," Nancy added.

The fact that Markus mentioned both Mesmer and Randleman was disturbing to Gary Zimmerman. Markus told him about everything that happened in relation to the blackouts and flashbacks.

"Someone possibly had placed psychic blocks on a number of these kids. Maybe when Markus starts recalling the events, we will get a clear picture of what is inside his mind. The fact or fiction could be from his own imagination or actual things he vaguely recalls seeing and hearing. It can be anything, any number of scenarios. Maybe even a different set of scenarios I know nothing about."

"I don't understanding any of this," Markus told him.

"I don't either," Nancy added.

"Let me try to explain. Bear in mind, I do know a thing or two about hypnotism, and the mind. But I'm no expert though Nancy thinks I am," Gary Zimmerman started his explanation. "People have been entering hypnotic-type trances for thousands and thousands of years. Different forms of hypnosis played a role in many cultures' religious practices, and still do. But the scientific concept of hypnotism wasn't conceived until the late seventeen hundred's."

"Franz Mesmer can be called the father of modern hypnotism. He was an Australian physician who believed hypnosis to be a mystical force flowing from the hypnotist into the subject. He believed it was magic and referred to it as animal magnetism. Many critics quickly dismissed the magical element. All things related to hypnosis are mostly theory, even now. Mesmer's assumption that the power behind hypnosis was magic not tinkering with the subconscious mind, has governed what most people believed to be true for some time. Hypnosis was originally called mesmerism, after Mesmer."

"What the hell is this, a history lesson, huh?" Markus blurted.

"Hypnotism was developed way before me and you. I guess that makes it history." Gary answered.

"What about Randleman?" Markus asked.

"Ahhh," Gary Zimmerman structured. "Randleman, Fritz Roy Randleman. He was a great illusionist and magician. There is a belief that Fritz Roy Randleman is a stage name. I've done extensive research on him, and if Fritz Roy isn't his first name then Randleman is definitely the last. He was born in Germany, and performed his tricks at a very young age in various traveling circuses, and gypsy fairs throughout Europe in the forty's and fifty's. Randleman was a hero of mine when I was a little boy because his tricks were so good they were believed to be actual magic. He allegedly died of old age in the early ninety's. He would have been close to eighty years old when he passed. I saw him perform his infamous Lord of the Flies trick in France when I was sixteen while vacationing with my family."

"What does all of that mean?" Markus asked once Gary stopped talking.

"It means that whoever played with your mind has studied a great deal. It means I have a task ahead of me," Zimmerman answered.

Nancy didn't know why Gary didn't tell Markus about the orphanage, and the possible pedophile cases. He didn't mention the kids they found with no knowledge of who they were, or how they wound up at the orphanage. Zimmerman reached into his briefcase and pulled out a stopwatch.

"I don't think it'll take me long to relax you into a suggestive state. Afterwards I can't give you any promises that I can do anything else. You might begin to tell me things once I begin asking you questions, though I'm not sure of what I should ask you or what you might tell me. You could be telling me what you think is the truth and it could all be lies, something someone placed inside your head," Gary Zimmerman told Markus.

"Ask me about the flies," Markus urged. "And about Michelle…"

"I don't think this has anything to do with some women you met at a club. I'm not sure why you blacked out then, or why you began seeing things after you encountered her. I think this is deeper than that."

"I want you to start there. I don't care about deeper. All I care about is not blacking out anymore. And I wanna know who this Michelle is. If you get my meaning…?" Markus was blunt. "I don't care about Mesmer or Randleman, but I do care about blacking out again. I do not like these dreams and these flies buzzing around inside my brain."

"Fair enough, I wouldn't like flies buzzing around inside my head either. Shall we begin?"

Markus took a deep breath. "Ready when you are," he grinned nervously. "Be gentle."

Zimmerman laughed then his demeanor changed. He made Markus and Nancy switch seats. Now Markus was in the shrink position and Nancy was on the couch. He told Markus to sit as still as possible.

"Concentrate on sitting as straight as you can, keep your eyes on this…" Zimmerman said, allowing the timepiece to begin spinning back and forth— forth and back.

Dr. Adler's eyes were glued to the stopwatch. Minutes passed and she had no knowledge of time. Her eyes never blinked. She gasped as she felt relaxation. She realized she had been mesmerized by the stopwatch like Markus was being beguiled. Nancy shook off whatever was causing her to relax. She gathered her wits and gave the timepiece Zimmerman was spinning in Markus's face a better look and saw that there were initials engraved on it… F.R.R…

27

"Who is Michelle?" Markus asked once he came back to his senses. "Nancy, did Gary find out who she is?"

He felt like he emerged from the deepest darkest void. He remembered nothing but the back and forth motion of the timepiece Zimmerman had dangled in front of his face. It was going back and forth and forth and back, Zimmerman was talking to him with the smoothest voice, telling him to relax.

He relaxed instantly. One moment he was watching the timepiece, the next moment he was staring into Nancy's face. He completely lost track of time. Markus didn't know how long he was under hypnosis.

Dr. Adler looked like she saw a unicorn or something beyond the norm. She was staring at Markus and he deduced that he was hypnotized for a while.

"I think you believe Michelle is the little girl you've being seeing when you first began seeing what I think was a fabricated flashback. In other words, I don't think it's a true piece of your past. She might quite possibly have been another kid involved in what I believe is called the Randleman Protocol but I'm not sure. Michelle might be a person you were in an emotional situation with during your ordeal, when you were a child. She might be a made up character in your mind."

"What protocol? What ordeal?" Markus asked.

Zimmerman appeared to be as tired as Markus. He looked over at Markus, who wanted to go and get some sleep, but he wanted to get to the bottom of this.

"Why can't I remember the session?"

"Which shall I answer first, your first, second question or the third?" Zimmerman asked.

"The third," Dr. Adler said.

Markus and Zimmerman turned their attention to her.

"Sorry," she said.

"I don't know why you can't remember our extremely long conversation. You were very talkative. I think whoever hypnotized you, or was hypnotizing you placed a series of defense mechanism inside your mind, called the Randleman Protocol. The Randleman Protocol is triggered when the rational portion of your mind starts situating the facts from the fiction they placed in your brain."

"I don't understand any of this," Markus said, glancing at the wall.

It was a few minutes past one in the morning. He had been under hypnosis for more than four hours.

"What happened to me when I was a kid?" He asked.

"I think you were kidnapped, or put up for adoption. I'm only speculating because I've known about something similar, an old case I was working on when I was a detective in the missing persons division. You have experienced a situation that involves an orphanage, or your time in the orphanage is false memory. Jonathan Manners indeed purchased you. I'm sure of this but from whom, I don't know. Your rational mind can't accept that you saw Jonathan walking before because the memory is false. Someone created your first encounter with Jonathan and Gwyneth through hypnosis." He paused to think about things. "It's only logical to assume that Gwyneth told you the truth. There are other children involved. Michelle most likely was possibly one of them, or she reminds you of someone you experienced the ordeal with. I know of six other persons besides you who were possibly in the same situation. I wasn't able to thoroughly examine them like I did you. I think you were sold, I think all the kids were put up for fake adoptions. I think the program involved or involves giving a child a bogus identity and reprogramming their thought process through hypnosis so when they get older they will excel in a specific field or situation. All of this is very strange. I'm going to get to the bottom of this."

Gary Zimmerman seemed incensed by this. Markus wanted to put everything behind him. Knowing more about his situation served to confuse him even more. It was like he was living some perverse science fiction he didn't understand, and wasn't sure if he even wanted to. He wanted to ask more questions. Markus wanted to know about his past. He wanted to know what else Zimmerman knew. Markus was scared.

"Do you think Michelle has flashbacks and blackouts?" Nancy asked.

Markus gave her a weird glance. He was going to ask Gary

Zimmerman the same question.

"No," Gary said matter of fact. He seemed confident in his answer. "I think Markus was reprogrammed, and the reprogramming included this Randleman Protocol. Markus I think, you were hypnotized for one specific reason then you were put under Randleman's watch again." He held up the stopwatch he used to hypnotize Markus. He offered it to him, but Markus refused to touch it. He put the timepiece inside one of his pants pockets. "I suspect the Randleman Protocol is the reason why you were having flashbacks and blacking out. Randleman or someone who practices his method fumbled. He or she shouldn't have attempted to rewrite what had already been rewritten. Your mind was undergoing some sort of healing, attempting to regenerate itself back to its normal state fighting the protocol. That is why you've been blacking out I think. You're mind didn't understand what was going on, what was the truth and what was the lie. So your mind would shut down. You are so old now. Initially I think you were first introduced to hypnosis when you were ten years old. The Randleman protocol might have been added when you were much older."

"Why do you suspect these things?" Markus asked.

"Because in the beginning you spoke to us with child-like adolescence," Dr. Adler answered before Zimmerman could. "Then as the session progressed your speech and mannerisms matured. I estimated the age to be nine or ten in the beginning and then possibly fourteen or sixteen years old."

"Why would anyone wanna do this to me?" Markus asked, shaking his head.

"I don't know. I think you were originally hypnotized and psychically implanted with information that would urge or compel you to become some sort of athlete when you got older if you were guided in that direction. But that never happened. I think Randleman tried to wipe that out and put something else there. I think the first person who was supposed to purchase you reneged for some reason and whoever is behind this got another customer. Only that customer wanted you to possibly become something else. I know, it all sounds so damn strange, some sort of modern day slavery, something out of the *Twilight Zone*."

"An athlete…?" Markus repeated to himself singling that out above everything else.

"I asked you about various things. I began asking you about sports, and when I mentioned football you said things I honestly feel you shouldn't know. Maybe you're a sports buff but why were you able to recite hundreds of plays, you know everything about the game, and you know things that only a physical therapist or physical trainer should know. Think Markus. You've never played football in your life, any sport for that matter. You've never been taught anything about physical therapy or nutrition. Why do you know so much? Think."

Markus mind whirled into overdrive. Zimmerman was right. He had things in his mind he never knew he had. Situations, he saw himself in sports scenarios. It was all about football and it was all in his brain. Markus thought about the drink he whipped up. The protein drink he would consume before he did sex on film. Where did he get the formula from? It was something only athletes drank. Something only a nutritionist would prescribe to improve stamina.

"Damn!" He uttered, shaking his head. "I'm in the wrong line of work. I should be in the NFL instead of in the adult film industry."

He thought about how much he knew about the female anatomy, about the Karma Sutra, about G-spots and the clitoris. He had a lifetime of information in his mind about sports and sex and he hadn't the foggiest idea where it came from. "Was my programming of a sexual nature as well?" He asked.

Zimmerman nodded his head.

"Either your programming, or your reprogramming. I think the person who messed with your brain tried to erase one but couldn't. Now you have a whole bunch of stuff inside your mind." He saw an expression of uncertainty form on Markus's face. "Don't worry," he assured him. "Most people don't use as much as ten percent of their brain capacity in their lifetimes."

"So I'm okay now, I'm cured?" Markus asked.

"Slow down," Zimmerman began. "I wouldn't say you're cured. But I don't think you'll be blacking out anytime soon."

"If I wasn't cured I'd have blacked out thinking about all of this. All of this is fucking weird. If you get my meaning…?" Markus thought about his own words completely forgetting about what Gary had stated. He looked at Nancy with wide eyes. "I'm cured."

"How do you know?" She asked.

"I'm thinking about all these sexual positions that are now at the focal point of my mind. Shit, I never knew what a focal point was till now. I'm thinking about how Michelle will look and feel in something called the spinal crab."

Zimmerman laughed as loud as anyone could.

He was so excited he left with little to no concern about all the other things Gary Zimmerman had discovered while he was under hypnosis. Gary told him he surmised so many things and with the information he had and a few leads he would be able to figure out more.

Markus told him to give him a call when he found anything

worth mentioning, anything that wasn't jumbled up with hypnosis and mental hocus pocus. He didn't want to hear anymore about reprogramming and his subconscious mind and this Randleman Protocol. He was glad he wouldn't be blacking out again.

He wanted to get to know Michelle. He kept thinking about how he used to blackout every time he thought of her. Now he had Michelle on the brain and wasn't feeling dizzy. He wasn't going to blackout the next time he encountered her. The fact that she might be a victim of some mind reprogramming conspiracy like him mattered little. He was going to call her as soon as he walked out of Nancy Adler's office then he realized how late it was. Markus planned on calling her tomorrow. Downstairs, he hailed a cab.

"Wait," Dr. Adler shouted before he hopped inside the cab. "Markus you left my office so abruptly." She began.

"Nancy it's Thursday already, I've been under hypnosis for the past four hours. Don't you think I've had enough for one night?" Markus said irritably. He realized his tone and simmered down. "I'm sorry. I'm just tired that's all."

"No, I apologize. You have been through so much the past couple of days, weeks, months; your whole life. I'm being very insensitive," she yawned. Markus contracted the yawn. "We are both tired," she smiled.

"I'll call you," he said and hopped in the cab.

Before the door completely closed Nancy said, "Your therapy isn't over yet. I'm not through with you Mr. Excitement. I want to see you Monday at six p.m. sharp."

"Our agreement was for three sessions. I would say I'm not obligated to deal with you in a professional manner anymore, Dr. Adler." She didn't know what to say to him after he said that. She grinned when he said, "I will agree to a date on Monday. I would love

28

to see you before my trip to the Orient."

When Markus arrived at Sparks's apartment, Sparks wasn't home. Entice let him in. She greeted him at the door in red ruffled panties, perky nipples and nothing else. Markus didn't understand why she was always around. She was doing her toe nails when he rang the bell and waddled to the bedroom after letting him inside.

Entice didn't seem to have any interest in anything besides her pedicure. She didn't ask Markus about his day, about his car or about the hypnosis session. He was so tired all he had an interest in was going to sleep.

He went to couch in the living room and went to sleep. His whole life was one big *Twilight Zone* episode. Everything from being sold like some sort of product to Jonathan Manners, and handed to Gwyneth as a birthday present, to people playing around with his head, and rewriting his memory, placing all forms of information inside his brain. Everything was way too much for him to intake in one day.

Markus awoke and wasn't surprised to find out he had slept twenty-four hours. Once he picked his head off the sofa, Entice and Sparks greeted him. Markus ran to the bathroom to take one of the longest pisses of his life.

"I'm starving," he announced when he walked out of the bathroom.

"Your black ass slept for over twenty-four hours!" Sparks snapped like it was his fault. "I tried to wake you and that was like waking a damn corpse."

"Today is Friday or something?" Markus asked, sounding confused.

"Yeah Friday or something," Sparks answered with annoyance. "Sleeping that much is bad for business, we gotta go check out the place Tee-Neck is renting to us."

Markus grimaced. He wanted to snap at Sparks and tell him that managing his porn career wasn't managing his life. Then he thought about his porn career. He used to have an agent, but he didn't need anyone governing his life. Markus knew that wasn't the truth. He thought about Jonathan Manners and Gwyneth and how they used to control his life. Sparks seemed like a friend but so did Tanisha. He didn't know who he could trust. He was way too hungry to argue or consider things further. He had Michelle on his mind. With every situation presenting itself he decided to take a shower and get dressed. As he dressed Markus thought about his car.

"I gotta go see about my car," he announced to no one in particular. Sparks and Entice were all ears.

"I thought you handled that the other day."

"Something else came up. Listen Sparks, I have a whole lot of issues, things beyond my career, my living arrangements, and Tanisha and Cali."

"No one knows this better than my black ass do," Sparks said with more annoyance. "I'm here to help you, buddy." His disposition softened. "You need me Markus. I need you. You're making me see life in a whole new spectrum. Now that I manage you and Entice, I don't have to be out on the streets selling drugs as much."

"Oh…" Markus said.

"Don't think I'm here to be another issue in your life. I got big plans for your black ass, for us. While you did the *Snow White* beauty sleep routine, I got you a photo opportunity."

"A photo opportunity…?" Markus asked, confused. "What do you mean by that?"

"I mean publicity. There is this magazine called *Porno Industry*. It's like *Rolling Stone Magazine,* but its porn instead of rock n roll and music. I got you on the cover."

Markus heard of the magazine. He knew there was a lot of racism in the porn industry. He never saw a black man on the cover of the magazine.

"How did you manage to get me on the cover?"

"Never mind that," he answered with a grin. "We leave for Japan next Thursday and the photo-shoot is set up for Wednesday twelve noon. They wanna interview you, you and Daisy Lace." He looked over at Entice. She was sitting down, looking cute, watching the two of them talk. "I tried to get Entice on the cover with you, but they said she wasn't a known name. But they heard of you. They know all about your black ass. They wanna put you and Daisy Lace on the cover."

"Daisy Lace… Have you contacted Daisy?"

"Yeah, I've been using your phone while you were sleep. I've been getting to know all the people associated with your career. Daisy agreed. Daisy was a big porn star two or three years back till her white ass decided to strictly work off-camera."

"I know all this," Markus laughed. Sparks never ceased to amaze him. "You can tell me more about this magazine cover once I've gotten some breakfast."

"After breakfast we gotta go straight to Jersey to see about that house. Some dude named Petey is gonna meet us there with the keys. It's already furnished."

"I know," he said to his new manager and friend. "I've done movies in the backyard of that place. It's huge."

"Petey said it's a mansion," Entice blurted excitedly.

Markus took a look at Entice and grimaced. He was about to accept the fact that he was stuck with Sparks, but hadn't considered being stuck with her. Entice was a very attractive girl he fucked, but that was for the cameras. The only woman Markus had ever slept with out of any affection and not due to necessity and or some business arrangement was Tanisha. He took a very deep breath and let it out slowly.

"Let's go." He said to his new roommates. "Let's get settled into our new home."

After eating a huge breakfast at a diner in Brooklyn, they hopped inside Sparks's car and rushed to Jersey. The place Tee-Neck agreed to rent to Markus was a huge house with five bedrooms, three living rooms, one humongous kitchen and dining room, and five and a half bathrooms. There was a lot of land outback and an NBA sized basketball court with an Olympic sized swimming pool. Sparks and

Entice were instantly amazed.

Petey, Tee-Neck's very fat Italian friend, walked them around the place. Markus didn't need the grand tour. He had already been throughout the house. Instead of following them, he excused himself. Markus went out to the back of the house, sat down on a chair near the pool and whipped out his cell phone. He decided to call Michelle. The anticipation was killing him. It was like he was hypnotized all over again, hypnotized because he couldn't stop thinking about her.

The phone rang four times before Michelle answered, "Who is this?" She asked suspiciously.

Her voice was raspy, it was very distinctive. He grinned. He loved her voice already. This was the first time he actually heard her speak. "Hello," she said again. Markus didn't know what to say. "Speak!" She yelled. "Speak before I hang up."

"Ah, Michelle," he said.

"Yes. Who else would answer my phone?" She snapped, "Who is this?"

"Markus," he replied. "Markus Johnson."

"Doesn't ring a bell," she told him. "You might have the wrong number."

"Didn't I ask for Michelle? I'm sure this is the correct number. I just gave you the wrong name."

"So give me the right one," Michelle said in a sweet voice.

Markus smiled at his phone. He didn't know exactly how to approach this. He figured she would know him as Mr. Excitement so he gave her that name. "It's Mr. Excitement," he said, feeling stupid.

"Oh," Michelle's vocal expression changed instantly from casual flirtation to annoyance. "You...!"

Markus grimaced. Her tone reverberated through his brain like a long echo. He heard it over and over. Markus was not aware of the sort of information Tanisha passed on to Michelle, and wasn't about to call Tanisha to inquire. He didn't know what Michelle knew about him, or about his situation. He never dealt with woman outside his perverse circle of sex, whether Gwyneth, her friends and associates, or the porn stars he fucked on film.

There was a deafening silence for about a minute then Michelle asked, "What do *you* want?"

"I wanna see you," he said, figuring that wasn't the best thing to say.

"For what…?" She asked. "Why do you want to see me?"

Good question, he thought. He wasn't quite sure why he wanted to see her. Perhaps just to look at her gorgeousness and gaze into her eyes.

"Do you watch the Science Fiction channel?" He asked completely turning the conversation in another direction.

"Excuse me?" Michelle blurted.

"You ever saw an episode of *Twilight Zone*, or read a Stephen King novel?"

"Why?" She asked. "What the fuck does this have to do with anything?"

"Meet me later and I'll tell you."

"Fuck no!" She began laughing on the other side of the phone. "You're that crazy guy who faints all the time."

"You ever dream of flies?" He asked.

Michelle hung up the phone.

Markus, Sparks and Entice were out on the back patio having lunch with Petey. Petey was fat and humorous and reminded Sparks of

Dom DeLuise. Petey was an accomplished chef. Starting the propane grill out back, he put some meat on it with his special herbs and spices in a small shaker he pulled out of his pocket.

He told them it was freshly picked herbs and spices he got from his own dear mother in Sicily. Sparks wondered what sort of man carried around his own herbs and spices, obviously a fat one, he deduced.

Entice found a portable radio inside the house and brought out back. She began dancing the way a video hoochie would providing entertainment for the men. Music played, they ate, talked and watched her dance.

Sparks asked Markus about his recent visit to the psychiatrist. Markus told him the whole story from what happened at Gwyneth's to what Gary had found out while he was under hypnosis.

Sparks said, "I'm not gonna say I understand any of this or believe most of it. But I've seen you blackout with my very own eyes. Once I saw…" He let his words linger.

"What, what is it?" Markus asked. "You can tell me. Once you saw what?"

"It's nothing," he dismissed, wanting to change the subject. "You were gonna tell me something about Michelle."

"Sparks, if you got something you wanna talk about you can tell me. It can't be as crazy as what I've told you."

"True," he said. "I think I seen a flying saucer once."

Markus and Entice broke out in heavy laughter.

"Fuck you!" Sparks snapped. "You and your, fucking Randleman Machine or Protocol or whatever…"

"Come on Sparks," Markus said once he settled down. "I wouldn't even believe myself if I weren't living my own life." Sparks gave Markus a dirty look. "Shit, if it wasn't for Gwyneth's very own words and Nancy and Gary Zimmerman's psychological mumbo jumbo…"

"Back when I was around twelve or thirteen years old in the old country," Petey began taking the time to stop eating to tell his tale. "I saw what could have only been a UFO."

"An unidentified flying object," Entice uttered. "I saw this show on channel five about UFO's. They showed all forms of video taped stuff. And I read somewhere about how aliens from other planets beam cows up onto their flying saucers and use their blood like lotion for their green scaly skin."

It was Sparks turn to laugh. "Lotion for their green ass scaly skin…? Life forms from other planets have eczema, is that it?"

"I saw all forms of lights, they weren't planes, no plane could zip in and out and up and down like them. One got real close, I saw it with my own eyes, it was metal, disk shaped and smooth, smooth like chrome finish," Petey said, and began eating again.

"What were you saying about Michelle?" Sparks decided to get back to the original subject.

"She hung up on me after I mentioned flies," Markus said.

"She probably thinks your black ass is crazy. Some bitches ain't into crazy niggas."

"Nah, I think she hung up because she dreams about flies like me, and like anyone else who's been under the Randleman Protocol," Markus said, sounding serious.

"I don't know if she was in this crazy weird hypnosis, child kidnapping, and slavery situation with you, and was programmed or reprogrammed with some sort of stopwatch and or this Randleman machine. If she does see flies in her dreams and faints like you and has flashbacks…"

Markus interrupted Sparks, "Had flashbacks, I'm cured."

"Whatever," Sparks snapped. "If she has the symptoms you had, she'll call you back. She probably hung up from shock. She was like, how did he know I dream about flies. But if she doesn't call you back then she thinks you're a nut case. Either way, forget about her. We got more important things to worry about."

"Such as," Markus inquired. "What is more important than Michelle?"

"Ain't no bitch important at all," Sparks said looking over at Entice. "Present company excluded." He got back at Markus. "Your monthly medical checkup, and AIDS test, and your vehicle, I think those are priorities."

"Yeah, those are definitely priorities," Markus agreed.

"We got a meeting with Audra tonight."

"When did you speak to Audra?"

"Yesterday, while you were comatose. She's gonna sue you so I told her to meet up with us. I figured it would be better if we talked to her in person."

"Good idea," Markus felt like he needed an aspirin. If he didn't have a headache already he was about to get one soon.

29

After Markus went to see his primary doctor, Sparks drove him to Gwyneth's. He didn't even have to go upstairs. Sparks pulled up to the front of the building and Markus spotted his Lexus parked across the street. It was back to its original splendor. He walked inside the building and the door man went behind the desk and handed him the keys. The doorman told him Gwyneth Manners and Emily were gone for the day. Markus smiled.

The next time he saw Gwyneth, he would thank her for getting his car fixed before he killed her. Markus thought about Jonathan Manners's funeral. He was about to ask the doorman when it was. He figured he should get one last look at Mr. Manners if only to spit in his face before they lowered him six feet in the ground. So many things were revealed to Markus in such a short time. His immediate worries were his daughter Emily, Michelle, and of course Gwyneth's stability was always a worry, if not for him then for Emily's sake.

Markus told Sparks and Entice he would meet them at the lounge for the meeting with Audra at ten which was the time she specified.

"Keep your black ass out of trouble," Sparks warned.

"You do the same," Markus said and they went their separate ways.

His cell phone rang while he drove. He pulled it out and looked at the caller ID. It was Tanisha. Markus was about to answer it but the urge wasn't as strong as his anger. "Fuck her!" He said, pressing the ignore button.

Tanisha called again and Markus let the phone ring itself out this time. He wasn't going to get drawn back into anymore bullshit. He was finally getting some form of control over his life. Gary Zimmerman had cured his blackouts and a veil had been lifted from his mind.

Markus began forming a plan for his life while he drove. He figured he would do fuck films until his contract with Smut Central Entertainment ended. If he could invest some of his money wisely; he could get out of the business completely.

He was compelled to indulge in sex more because of the hypnosis and the Randleman situation than from anything else. Now he felt he could combat that urge by using the whole hypnosis situation. He could become a sport commentator with all the knowledge he had of football, turning a negative into a positive.

He didn't care about where he came from, or what kind of past he had before he was kidnapped and hypnotized, or even how he became a specimen for this *Twilight Zone* shit and why.

It was late Friday afternoon. His daughter was somewhere

with her crazy mother, and he was thinking about Michelle. Things were getting better for Markus Johnson because he was not about to blackout.

Gary Zimmerman stood in front of Gwyneth Manners's building two hours before she and Emily hopped out of a chauffeur driven Benz with a handful of shopping bags. Zimmerman spotted the woman he assumed was Gwyneth, based on Nancy's description. He took a final pull from the cigarette he was smoking, flung it down and stomped it out.

Before walking to the front door of her building, she quickly dialed on her cell phone. After a few words, the doorman came outside and grabbed Emily by the hand, walking her inside the building.

Zimmerman arched an eyebrow in curiosity. The doorman had disappeared inside when Gwyneth walked over to him and said, "How many of you guys are going to interrogate me in one day. Isn't there a law against this?"

"I don't know," Zimmerman answered with uncertainty. Then he said, "Are you Gwyneth Manners?"

"Yes I am," she said, sounding quite annoyed. "Why don't you guys just take a picture and pass it around. That way you don't have to ask me such a stupid question. Can't I mourn my husband's death in peace?"

Zimmerman smiled. Nancy had told him Gwyneth was quite an unusual woman. He was inclined to agree. She was carrying so many bags she could barely hold them all and still the chauffeur was unloading a trunk filled with more bags.

"Does shopping help you mourn?" Zimmerman asked.

"Maybe it does," she snapped before she said. "Hey, fuck you! Just ask your questions and leave. I've got things to do."

"Fine," he said. "How long have you known Markus Johnson?"

"Huh?" She was taken back by the question. "This isn't about my husband's death?"

"No," he said with all out confusion. "Are you a murder suspect?"

"Do you have another cigarette?" She asked taking a better look at Zimmerman before saying, "You're handsome in a *Moonlighting, Bruce Willis* sort of way."

"Well I'm a private investigator, but I don't work for the *Blue Moon Detective Agency.*"

Gwyneth laughed. He handed her a cigarette then pulled out a lighter, and gave her a light. She took a long drag on the cigarette before speaking.

"You mentioned Markus. Did he hire you?"

"Indirectly, I would have to say," Zimmerman said and lit a cigarette for himself.

Her hands shook as she smoked and frown-lines showed through her makeup. Gwyneth's a nervous wreck Gary thought. Dr. Adler had informed him about her mental issues. He figured it wouldn't take long for a person like her to crack and start singing. He let her smoke.

"I want to find out how you were introduced to Markus." Before she could spit out her lie he added, "I want to know where Jonathan Manners purchased Markus, from where or and from whom."

She nearly choked on the last bit of the cigarette. The cigarette fell from her mouth to the ground.

"I told Markus that he was purchased while he was choking

me to death. I said whatever I had to say for him to get off of me," she started crying. "My whole world is crumbling down all around me."

Zimmerman frowned. "I took a couple of drama courses in college," he told her.

"Huh?" Tears were streaming down Gwyneth's face.

"You're a terrible actress. Listen, I'm not here to arrest you or anything like that. I couldn't arrest you if I wanted to anyway. I just want some honest answers."

Gwyneth tears stopped and she cut her performance in mid sob. She calmly glanced at him before she said, "Be a dear and help me with these bags. I'll have the maid order us something to nibble on."

Markus was purposely late arriving at the lounge. Audra and Sparks were sitting on adjacent love seats arguing, when he entered. Entice was at the bar drinking an apple Martini and chatting with some white dude who was obviously trying to pick her up. Markus wanted to walk over to the bar and join them. He figured their company would be less stressful than Audra and Sparks.

He had to deal with Audra and eventually walked over. "What are you two drinking? I'm ordering the next round."

"Save your money traitor. You'll need all the money you can muster for legal fees," Audra barked, taking the time to stop yelling at Sparks to yell at him.

"I'll have a Jack and Coke. She'll have a Cosmo," Sparks said to Markus.

"Don't be telling anyone what the fuck I'm having," she fumed.

Audra seemed genuinely furious. Markus had never seen her pissed off like this before.

"After arguing with you for the last half hour, I would say I know you well enough. I know your ass is a bitch," Sparks smiled after the comment.

Markus grimaced wondering what Sparks had said to make Audra angrier, if that was possible.

"Audra," Markus said, sitting next to her. "I've already decided to keep you as my agent."

"What?" Sparks said shocked. "She'll be another expense."

"Another expense that *we* can afford, you're my manager. I'm sure you'll situate more business for us. Audra got me this far, I'm sure she'll get me even further."

He smiled at himself. This was getting a hold of his life and directing himself. This was what Zimmerman had done when he entered his head, and revealed what he did. He gave Markus some much needed strength.

"I wanna go with you guys to Japan," Audra said to him.

"Done," he said, looking over at Sparks. "See that she gets a ticket on the same flight as us, and see about hotel arrangements."

Sparks was about to protest but Markus quickly added, "She's a part of the team."

"I've always been. I started this damn team." Audra leered at Sparks and continued. "What sort a name is Sparks, anyway?"

"Markus was right," Sparks said, whipping out a recently rolled blunt from inside a pocket.

Sparks lit the marijuana. Audra and Markus knew smoking indoors and in a public place was quite illegal in New York. And what he was smoking was even more illegal. They don't call him Sparks for nothing. He would spark up anywhere.

"Markus was right about what?" Audra asked after two or three minutes. Sparks had stretched her patience.

"I forgot," he said absentmindedly then he took another puff on the blunt and passed it to Markus. "But his black ass was right. I'm quite certain of it."

30

The weekend came and went for Markus Johnson. It was a weekend with surprises, one of his better weekends. He spent it with his daughter. She had a great time at his new home in Jersey. Jonathan Manners's funeral was on Sunday. Emily didn't have a clue of his death. Gwyneth felt it wasn't necessary to tell her.

He didn't know how to introduce a subject like death to his daughter. He pondered it up to the point where he went to Gwyneth's early Saturday morning to get Emily. Once she was in his arms, he forgot all about Jonathan Manners and his demise.

He drove to his new home and introduced Emily to Sparks and Entice. Emily found Sparks quite humorous, and Entice instantly became a willing babysitter. Whenever Emily wanted something or was curious about anything, she asked Entice. Markus smiled at that.

Now he knew why he had Entice in his life.

They were going to have a huge cookout Saturday night, a sort of Smut Central Entertainment bash for Mr. Excitement since he was exclusively and officially signed to them.

Tee-Neck had arranged everything. After Markus and Emily got settled in, the hired help started coming, caterers, waiters, bartenders, carpenters, audio engineers, and valet parkers. Emily enjoyed every minute of it. Sparks began directing things. The party was scheduled to officially start at ten. Audra arrived two hours early.

Sparks grimaced when he opened the door and saw Audra. She walked in with a pair of Chanel shades on, looking around the capacious and lavishly furnished home of Markus Johnson.

"How much did Tee-Neck give you?" She asked when she found Markus out back by the pool.

"Meet my daughter, Emily." Markus said, ignoring the question.

"She's such a lovely girl," Audra said without even looking at the smiling Emily. "Isn't this the place you filmed *Ass Bangers Volume 22*?"

"Yes," he grimaced. "Audra," Markus said, pointing down.

"Oh," Audra said, pushing her shades up to get a better view. "Oh, I'm sorry Markus. Who is this again?"

"Emily," the little girl answered. "I'm daddy's daughter."

"What a cutie you are," Audra smiled.

By the time midnight hit, the party was jumping in earnest. Hundreds of people were in attendance, industry insiders mostly. Markus only knew about thirty of the guests. He had fucked quite a few of the women on film, and met a few casually at some shoot or another.

Just after midnight, Entice put Emily to sleep in one of the guest rooms. Sparks was very suspicious of everyone besides the female porn stars. He had got some business cards whipped up and was handing them out like they were condoms.

"I manage Mr. Excitement," he said. "We're doing big things. You need to jump on board."

Sparks chatted with Daisy Lace and Markus grinned at them. He knew Daisy was easy to talk to and he figured Sparks was trying to persuade her to let Entice in on some of the bigger films. Markus had to give Sparks credit for working all the angles. His manager had to have chit chatted with everybody at the party. Everyone in the place had a business card from Sparks. His business cards were on every table, they were even being used as coasters.

Vonchell made her entrance at one a.m. She walked in with a Brazilian woman who looked as edible as she did. Vonchell had on the sheerest light green dress anyone had ever seen, it was so thin her body showed like she wasn't wearing anything at all. It looked like it was made of gossamer strands, and spiders had spun it.

Vonchell kicked off her sandals and said, "Walking barefoot is good for my aura." She explained to Tee-Neck. "It brings you closer to the earth and nature."

"Excitement," Tee-Neck yelled when he saw him.

Markus turned toward the voice, saw Tee-Neck then he saw Vonchell and grimaced. He wasn't fond of her, but had to admit Vonchell was the hottest looking thing at the party. She was the most gorgeous woman he worked with on film.

He walked over to them. "What's going on, Tee-Neck?"

"Hey, Mr. Excitement," Vonchell said, eyeing Markus like

meat.

She looked at her Brazilian companion and said, "This is the one with the humongous dick I was telling you about, the one who fainted on me."

"And you are," Markus said, extending his hand to Vonchell's sexy looking companion, and ignoring Vonchell completely.

"Mango," She told him giving him her delicate hands. "They call me Mango."

"You should try her Mr. Excitement. She really does tastes like one," Vonchell said with a killer's coldblooded smile.

"Maybe one day I will," Markus told her. He was looking at Mango when he spoke.

"I want you to stay as close to Vonchell as possible. I got media people here and when they take pictures, you two better be together," Tee-Neck scoffed.

"Why?" Markus asked.

"Because you two are going to be the biggest adult entertainers in the world soon. The scripts Daisy Lace wrote are innovative. The movie you two are filming in Japan is going to make porn history. *Black Geisha* is a blockbuster feature film. Shit the budget is well over two million dollars. Porno doesn't cost that much to make. You guys are about to make history."

Vonchell put her slender arms around Markus and hugged up close to him.

"We're gonna make history together, Mr. Excitement. Tee-Neck says so." Vonchell saw a couple of media people moving closer toward them with cameras.

"Quick, Mango, get on the other side of Big Dick."

Before Markus could respond, Vonchell gave him a moistest kiss on a cheek and Mango did the same on the other side. "Say cheese!" She laughed, raising one of her beautifully athletic legs and leaning in. Cameras began flashing.

The party atmosphere escalated then began its decline. Mango was in almost every flick taken of Markus and Vonchell. He was quite sure that was exactly what Vonchell wanted. He didn't know what was going on and he didn't care. Markus was tired and wanted everyone to leave.

Most of the guests did leave but about a hundred people remained scattered, lingering about. The deejay was still playing music and there was an endless amount of food left. It was five a.m., Sunday morning. Markus was going to tell Sparks to get rid of everyone in a few minutes.

Markus was lounging on a chair as close to drunk as he'd ever been, Entice was on his lap finishing up a drink. She nudged him and pointed over at the other side of the backyard. Vonchell and camera friendly Mango was having a very deep conversation with Sparks.

"I really hope he doesn't start managing her," Markus said.

"Why?" Entice asked. "Vonchell is really pretty."

"Beautiful is a better word, breathtaking is even better. But a lot of beautiful things are deadly packages. Like most bright colored snakes and toads, the prettiest ones, are the more poisonous. If you get my meaning...?"

"Why would Vonchell wanna be poison to you?" She asked.

"Maybe she doesn't, but she seems like trouble. She's very intelligent. Intelligence brings a certain danger. You keep your eyes on her."

"I ain't into girls, Markus. I mean on film yeah, but that's only business."

"Just keep your eyes on her anyway," he snapped with a smile. "I gotta go check on Emily."

Entice sitting on his lap was getting his dick hard.

"I'll go see about Emily," she said jumping up. "I got your girl," she said.

"Thanks," Markus said, kissing Entice on the lips.

"I'm getting out of here," Audra said. He turned and saw her sitting on a lounge chair behind him. "I'll keep my eyes on Vonchell."

Markus realized Audra heard every word he had spoken to Entice. He wasn't sure what to think about that.

"What do you think? Do you think I'm being paranoid? I mean, she's only a bitch right?"

"Bitches have caused whole civilizations to go down, Cleopatra, Delilah, and Joan of Arc..." Audra added. "She asked me to be her agent."

"And..."

"And, I know a good thing when I see it. None of you, I would hope want to stay in the porn business forever. I read a couple of Daisy Lace's scripts. Black Geisha is going to be a huge success. Shit, they are going to release a soft porn version that is getting an NR rating. This film is getting a lot of press and it has not even filmed yet. Why wouldn't I want to agent her? Once the next couple of films are released, you guys might actually do what no other adult entertainers have done in the history of the game."

"Which is?" He asked. He was far too drunk to ponder.

"Crossover into mainstream film and getting real acting gigs... Just think of how serious people will take you two, after you guys have been in a film with such a great script? And the historical relevance behind how much money Tee-Neck is putting behind this Black Geisha movie. He says two million is the budget but I think he's investing a whole lot more..."

31

Markus awoke late Sunday afternoon. He knew he wasn't alone. He attempted to rise out of bed but a body was atop him. It was Vonchell. Her lovely face was on his chest, eyes closed, sleeping ever so peacefully. Her sweet breath was blowing into his nostrils. He immediately flipped Vonchell off of him and to the floor. She hit the floor hard.

"Ouch!" She yelled still half sleep. "Hey!" Vonchell said rising off the floor.

Markus was getting out the bed. He would have stepped on her if she hadn't quickly moved out of his path.

Mango was deep in slumber at the foot of the bed. She was nude, sound asleep, snoring softly, looking satisfied and peaceful. He kicked her in her propped up ass and knocked her to the floor. Mango was roused out of sleep with pain.

"What the fuck!" she spoke with a heavy Brazilian.

"What the hell are you two doing in here?" He asked them.

"You don't remember Big Dick," Vonchell said with a laugh.

Mango got off the floor. He tried to situate his mind beyond the hangover. Markus remembered what happened. After Vonchell and Mango finished conversing with Sparks they walked over to him. They had drinks in hand and Markus drained both glasses. Then they escorted him to his room. He knew some sex had commenced afterwards.

Feeling woozy, he reached for his head, almost stumbling to the floor.

"You guys took advantage of me," he tried to yell, but his head wouldn't allow it.

"The way my pussy feels, I would say the advantage was all yours," Vonchell laughed.

Her eyes glinted with intelligence. She had the eyes of a snake, cold and calculating. She seemed like she had triumphed in some way. She was wallowing in Markus's confusion and anger.

"Most men are happy after being inside me."

"Get out!" He told them.

He would have forced them out but he was feeling dizzy. He almost blacked out and it would have been due to his hangover and nothing more. They were naked and looking beautiful. Markus wasn't sure about how he handled them in bed. His body was telling him he had entered at least one of the two.

Now all he wanted to do was take a shower. Markus wasn't sure why he was angry, but he was. It was one thing fucking a woman when he wanted or as a business situation on film. He didn't appreciate being molested, and taken advantage of. Markus had to laugh at himself.

A dude as big and sexual as me being taken advantage of, he mused. Sadly enough he had been taken advantage of his whole life. If not mentally then physically due to his fragile mentality, Markus was used to it. He had been drunk before and not felt the way he was feeling now. He wondered if Vonchell and Mango had slipped a Mickey in one of the drinks. He knew he shouldn't have been as woozy as he was. He didn't understand why Vonchell had made him her science project.

Once Vonchell and Mango left the room, he took a long shower. While he was inside the shower he thought about how even though Gary Zimmerman had hypnotized him and got a great deal of information out of him, he still couldn't recall his past. He felt like he was seeing the world through someone else's eyes. He had no idea how strange it felt until now.

Markus was easily manipulated, to the point where he hardly remembered doing the things he was asked to do. He was very submissive and agreeable, like a slave. He was the way he was programmed to be. He realized so many things were completely and utterly beyond his control. They didn't have to slip anything in his drink he was programmed to fuck on command.

He thought about Emily after he was dressed. It was almost four in the afternoon when Markus went to the room he had designated for his daughter. She wasn't there. Her bed had been made. Markus looked at the suitcase Gwyneth packed for Emily, and saw that she must have changed clothes. Markus searched the house.

He eventually found Emily in the kitchen with Entice. Entice was by the blender saying things that was making Emily laugh. They were blending what look like fruit smoothies. Emily saw her daddy and ran to him.

"Why do you sleep so much?" She asked.

Markus picked her up, and kissed her all over her face. He didn't bother to explain things.

"Did your mother call?" He asked. At six years old Emily already had a cell phone.

"Yes," she answered. "She said she's gonna pick me up at eight."

Markus let out a low moan. He didn't want Gwyneth knowing where he lived. That would only be a problem in the future. She never knew where he lived before. He decided not to think about it. He looked over at Entice. He was pretty sure she had given Gwyneth the address. He cursed silently, but didn't fault her one bit. It was his twisted life. And she was taking care of his daughter while he was drunk.

He asked Entice about Sparks's whereabouts. She told him Sparks departed as the last person left the party. He laughed. With all the women crawling around, all the hot looking porn personnel, and all the sexual possibilities, as woman hungry as Sparks seemed, he probably was in Brooklyn handling his drug business. Perhaps Sparks went to one of his baby's mother's houses.

He checked his cell phone and saw there were a few messages. Then he listened to them all. Tanisha left one begging him to call her. He erased it and acted like she had never left one. Nancy Adler left a message telling him she wasn't going to be able to attend the party. She also said Monday was a Jewish holiday and she wasn't seeing any clients. She wanted to meet during the day instead of the evening. Markus found that humorous. Nancy Adler was taking their meeting as a date. Good, he thought. He decided to call her after Gwyneth picked up Emily.

Gwyneth arrived at eight. Markus didn't want to see her face.

If he did he might have been compelled to choke her to death. He had no choice but to talk because directly after she arrived, he kissed his daughter goodbye and sent her to Gwyneth. But Gwyneth sent Emily to Valencia then she walked into the house.

"You seem to be doing well," she said, looking around. "This place is as big as the house in Los Angeles."

"The house Jonathan allowed you to accompany him to once," Markus laughed. "You were more of a slave to him than I could have ever been to you. You never loved him and he never loved you. You were both using each other."

"That's true. I guess he got the best of me, but I prevailed in the end." It was Gwyneth's turn to laugh. "I'm having that wonderful house he enjoyed in Los Angeles demolished." She began walking around the living room at her leisure looking at the paintings on the wall, occasionally touching a decoration. "You didn't furnish this place and neither did that ghetto looking bitch you have in here with you. Who did?"

"I don't know," he said honestly. "What the fuck do you wanna talk about bitch?"

"You move me when you call me that. I know you say it out of love," she purred.

"Get on with it and or get out, Gwyneth. It matters little to me."

"Why did you hire a private investigator?" She asked.

"How did you know?"

Gwyneth seemed confused. "You didn't send him to interrogate me about your situation?"

"My situation," he yelled.

He moved toward her. She gulped and reeled back. Markus saw genuine fear on her face. Seeing Gwyneth as scared as she looked pleased him, but it also made him feel disgusted with himself. He hated having a mean streak. He didn't like what he was becoming. He calmed down.

"You were in a worse situation than me. You needed someone you could take advantage of. You were worse off than I could have ever been being hypnotized or whatever."

"You're so right, Markus," she said with sadness. "Believe me when I tell you I never knew anything about hypnosis or this Randleman person. Jonathan left me in the dark. He was good at telling me nothing. Gary Zimmerman told me a few things and I told him all I knew. I was completely honest with him."

Markus watched her. She could and would never be completely honest with anyone, herself included. He didn't know what to ask her or what to say to her. He could always gather what Gwyneth told Gary Zimmerman but he wasn't sure if he wanted to pay the price. All he needed was a semblance of a relationship with her for the sake of his daughter. That was more than enough for him.

"How was the funeral?" He asked.

"It was the best funeral I've ever been to," she smiled. "You should've been there. We could've tossed our roses with a smile on our faces."

"Did you kill him?"

"Everyone's been asking me that," she said with a blank face.

"I wonder why?" He asked dryly.

"No," she finally answered, but didn't sound certain about the answer. "He was on his deathbed. And suppose I did. It wouldn't matter anyway, if the glove doesn't fit," Gwyneth jested.

"Get out of my house," he said in a not too nice of a tone. He had enough of Gwyneth. She was halfway toward the door when he asked one final question. "When are you gonna tell Emily about Jonathan?"

"When am I going to tell Emily that the devil is dead? I was hoping you would do that," Gwyneth said, walking out the door.

Markus cursed her under his breath.

32

Nancy Adler and Markus agreed to meet at Union Square Park on 14th Street at noon. The weather was going to be nice. She proposed they sit in the park and talk. Nancy promised to bring a picnic basket catered by her favorite neighborhood deli. She asked if he preferred a certain type or brand of wine. He said as long as it was alcohol he would drink it.

Markus wasn't sure what a picnic basket full of food and wine at a park in Union Square would be about. He had few dates with women he fucked on film, usually directly after work. After you had laid dick to a woman you just met, in front of two or three cameras, and in front of a half dozen people, romance wasn't an option. Markus Johnson wasn't sure what romance was. He knew he liked Nancy Adler. She was a person he could be completely honest with, and she was a person he knew for a fact wasn't his friend for some ulterior motive.

He figured the date with Nancy would be good practice for when he got acquainted with Michelle, if he ever did. He wasn't sure if Michelle wanted to hear from him again. She hung up on him.

"She probably thinks I'm crazy," he said aloud while he was driving to Manhattan. He lived a little over two hours from New York.

When he lived in Brooklyn it would have only taken him thirty minutes to reach Manhattan. He was sure the conversation with the shrink would be worth the distance. Besides the photo shoot on Wednesday, and a trip to Japan the day after that, there was nothing pressing.

Markus parked his car in a parking lot when he reached the Union Square area. He walked out the parking lot two minutes past noon. The park was three short blocks away. There was no need to rush. Time was something that never had much precedence over his existence.

Twenty-one years old as far as he knew. He should have asked Gary Zimmerman how old he was, Markus thought about his name. He was certain Markus Johnson was an adopted name. He still wasn't sure of what Gwyneth knew or didn't know. There were certain things on his mind since he underwent the session with Zimmerman. He neglected to ask.

After he was roused out of the suggestive state, he asked who Michelle was. It was like he could care less about anything in regards to himself but that wasn't so. He had no ability to focus on too many of his own concerns.

He was going to call Nancy and find out her exact location in the park, but after a couple of minutes he found her. Sitting on a bench under a tree, a wicker basket beside her, Nancy chose a great spot.

It was about seventy-five degrees with a light breeze, and lot of sunshine. The lid on the basket was closed, but Markus was sure there were a few treats inside. It looked big enough to hold a thanksgiving dinner.

"Why do you think I can't focus on things of relevance to myself? Do you think it has something to do with the programming?" Markus asked, walking to Nancy.

"No hello?" She asked, feigning disappointment with a halfhearted laugh. "Jesus, Markus."

"Sorry," he mumbled. "What do you think?" Markus asked, sitting down.

"You are way too much," Nancy laughed loudly then got into psychiatrist mode. "But if you truly want to know my assumption on the matter. I think perhaps you do have something inside your brain that suggests, encourages or urges you to be submissive."

He began asking more questions. "How can I end my submissiveness or combat it? Why wasn't Gary able to erase any of this?"

"Slow down," she said with a bit of volume. Markus paused, staring at her. "I'm starving. Can we eat before we play twenty-one questions?"

"Sorry," he said in a submissive tone. "Sure."

"Do you really want to eat or are you suggestively submissive?"

"I don't know. What do you think?" He said with a smile.

"You're taking your whole ordeal well. I imagine another person may go crazy after finding out what you did. Another person may ask more questions and want to find out more. After the session was over you seemed strangely uninterested in a number of things

Gary Zimmerman said."

"Nancy, the way my life has been, not blacking out anymore is such a triumph. I feel like I wanna know more, but then I could care less. I just wanna know if I honestly don't care or maybe something is making me not give a fuck. If you get my meaning…?"

"Have you contacted Michelle?"

"Yes…"

"And…" she probed. "What did she say? What did you say? Tell me all about it?"

"She hung up on me," Markus said with emphasis.

Nancy ignored his tone. "Why did she hang up?"

"This isn't one of your sessions. I ain't on your couch. I'm on a bench in a park. Didn't you say you were hungry? C'mon let's eat," Markus suggested.

Nancy Adler laughed then she spoke.

"Oh now let's eat huh. Listen Markus, I know this is a date and this isn't my office and this bench isn't the couch. But obviously you still have many issues and things to talk about. You're running with no more blackouts and flashbacks like that's the end of it all. You have suffered some major mental trauma. You might not realize it now but you have."

"You don't think I realize how serious shit is for me?" He exasperated.

"I didn't exactly say that. You know what, let's eat and talk about this some other time," Nancy said, opening the basket. "Want some wine?" She asked, pulling out the bottle and producing two wine glasses.

"Nancy you can't drink out in a park like this, in the middle of the day, in Manhattan," he said glancing around.

He was certain there were cops patrolling the park on the

regular.

"Of course I can," she said, laughing. "I'm white."

She handed Markus a corkscrew. He popped the bottle of wine. They ceased talking about any dilemma Markus was facing and concentrated on current events and cracking jokes while drinking wine. They ate lunch on the park bench.

Nancy found Markus entertaining and quite humorous. He had a soul that made him seem far beyond his years, though she knew determining his age was something that went along with determining so many things about Markus. Even with that she was pretty sure he was no older than twenty-one.

After lunch they went for a stroll through the park. Markus found himself strolling across the street to a shoe store. Union Square Park was surrounded by so many stores. He should have known it wasn't scientifically possibly for a woman to be around the area without at least window-shopping. Nancy did more than window shop. After she was all done, he was holding two out of the five shopping bags she had.

"Sorry," she began shuffling with all her bags. "I know this wasn't exactly what you expected the day to be."

"I've been out with a woman or two. I figured this was exactly how it was gonna turn out. If you get my meaning…?"

"Now let's get back to you," Nancy said.

"Oh…" he moaned.

"You didn't think I was going to let you get away that easy, did you?" she asked.

"Actually I did. I don't see a good reason to continue discussing me professionally until I return from my trip to the Orient."

"How long will you be in Japan?"

"For about four months. I'm doing two films. One called *Mr.*

Excitement Does Japan, I know it sounds corny. The other is called *Black Geisha*. That film has a great script. I might have to take a look at it before things get underway."

"You didn't even take a look at the script?" She laughed. "The flight to Japan is such a long one. You'll have more than enough time to skim through it."

"True," he said, laughing.

It was such a lovely day Markus and Nancy walked nearly thirty blocks talking, browsing through stores they found interesting, and enjoying each others company. Markus was so attracted to Nancy it scared him. He could tell that she felt the same way about him. Soon they found themselves a couple of blocks from where she lived in an upscale apartment high-rise. She told him where they were. He gave her a wicked grin and said, "Coincidence or fate."

"Coincidence," she blushed. "I feel like inviting you upstairs. But I know that wouldn't be a wise move."

"I know," he told her with honesty. "I would wanna indulge once we got upstairs."

He looked her over. She was the way she was usually dressed, very conservative. Her incredible frame made her look very much the opposite.

"I truly enjoyed the day," she told him.

Markus figured the date was at its end. Putting her bags down, she opened her arms wide for a hug. He moved in and accepted her embrace. She felt so warm. He moved a hand to her face and lifted her jaw with a finger. They looked into each others' eyes and kissed.

It was a slow, passionate kiss. Nancy moaned while his

tongue was probing inside her mouth. She had never been kissed the way Markus was kissing her. She welcomed his tongue. She felt between her legs getting hot and moist. Their bodies were connected. His enormous dick was poking her. She reached down and touched it, for a beat.

Then Nancy pushed away. She wasn't sure if she could take what he had to offer her physically, but was willing to try. Nancy was very certain he would be gentle with her.

"Come upstairs," she ordered.

"No," he said. "I respect you. You're too good for a guy who fucks on film."

"You're more than that, Markus. You are worth more than you think."

She knew what was going on. He was trying to see if he had a will of his own. Maybe he wasn't interested in sleeping with her. Nancy felt a bit foolish for making lust and lack of sex get the best of her. Her face turned red, she backed further away from him.

"You're right," he said, moving toward her as she was stepping away. "Wait," he told her and she stopped. He gave her another kiss, this time on the forehead. "We gotta do this again when I get back."

"Do what, almost make love?" She smiled.

"Oh," he snickered. "Is that what you think I do, make love? I fuck, Nancy."

"You wouldn't fuck me. You have more than sex programmed inside your head, Markus. I feel and sense much more. Monday's at eight p.m. for you. I'll continue working with Gary Zimmerman. We're going to find out exactly who you are under all the Randleman Protocol. More importantly, get you reacquainted with Michelle. If Gary Zimmerman's assumption is accurate you two are somehow connected. I hear the tone of your voice change when you say her name."

He took a long breath before saying, "Nancy, the tone of my voice changes when I say your name. Michelle used to make me blackout, you didn't. That's the only difference between you two."

Markus thought about saying something else, but didn't. He felt very awkward saying what he wanted to say and without saying it, he walked away.

She went up stairs and took a long, cold shower.

33

After Monday, the days went by swift and uneventful. Soon Wednesday presented itself and at noon, Sparks, Audra, Entice and Markus were in a warehouse with *Porno Magazine's* administrative staff. Susan Standings was the woman conducting the shoot. She was the editor in chief of the magazine. She told Sparks she hired a very talented photographer to help her team get good pictures of Daisy Lace and Mr. Excitement for the cover and inside of the magazine issue.

"She does great work with models and celebrities. She understudied with Rene Dupree. I rarely hire outside the magazine's personal staff, but this girl did a great photo spread of an R&B diva for a magazine called *On the Rise,* and it looked so-so sexy, I had to hire her," Susan Standing explained.

"Who the fuck is Rene Dupree…?" Sparks asked. "He sounds

like a faggot."

"Homosexual or not, he's a world renowned photographer," Susan said and immediately changed the direction of the conversation with a frown directed at Sparks. "Mr. Excitement's name is being spoken all over the adult entertainment circuit. We're very glad you contacted *Porno Magazine*. Daisy Lace is a treat. This won't be the first time she's graced our cover."

"Right," Sparks said giving her a fake grin. "Things look good here. Who thought up the visual schemes?" He was looking around the warehouse.

"The photographer, Michelle Watson, her ideas are so innovative, amazing."

There were so many things going on. A portion of the warehouse looked like a Japanese dojo fixed with an indoor stream filled with Japanese catfish, another portion of the warehouse was post modern gothic. It was a bedroom with a very large canopied bed covered with thick black Victorian sheets. The bed had huge lacquered posts, all the furniture in the room looked from the renaissance era. Every piece of furniture in the room was either too big or too small. It was odd but very creative and incredibly visual. Everyone was impressed and the place was buzzing.

Susan told Sparks they were shooting a number of sexually suggestive still photos of Mr. Excitement and Daisy Lace, together in both environments. Sparks asked about the interview. Susan asked if *Porno Magazine* could interview them on location while they were filming Black Geisha. Sparks didn't see why that couldn't happen.

Susan told him they would be busy for the whole day. Markus grimaced when he heard that part of the conversation. He hadn't packed for the trip yet. Sparks told him not to worry about it and encouraged him to pack light. "You can do some shopping when we get to Tokyo. Tokyo City is like Manhattan if not more congested, bigger and probably has more stores. Tokyo is the most expensive city in the world."

Though Susan had told Sparks the photographer's name and he relayed the information. Markus didn't put two and two together until the photographer walked into the warehouse.

He took one look at Michelle and almost blacked out. He wasn't sure if it was shock, or because of the Randleman Protocol but there she was looking like an angel gracing humanity with her presence.

Michelle was wearing a black wife beater and blue jeans. She had the same eyes and skin tone as Markus Johnson. She was taller than he figured she was. Markus had always envisioned her to be shorter. Michelle was even more gorgeous than he could have ever imagined.

She glanced around the warehouse, nodding with approving eyes. They had constructed the sets exactly the way she told them to. She spotted Markus Johnson as Susan Standings walked over to greet her. Michelle looked as if she was about to faint. She was shocked to see Mr. Excitement. Apparently she didn't know who she was going to photograph today.

She shook Susan's hand and smiled and waved at the rest of the *Porno Magazine* staff. Sparks looked over at Markus. Markus looked at him. Entice raised her brows without saying anything.

Markus gathered the nerve to walk over to Michelle while Susan was introducing her to Daisy Lace. Audra was on the sidelines observing everything with shrewd eyes. Sparks walked over to Audra and whispered something in her ear. Audra's eyes opened wider.

"And this is Mr. Excitement," Susan told Michelle.

"We've met," Michelle said dryly.

"That we have," he replied. "Hi Michelle," he said.

"Let's get things popping," Michelle snapped and turned away.

She carried two cameras. One was a small thirty-five mm digital and the other was a camera in a case that looked like it belonged in a museum. They went to the post modern set with the strange furniture and huge bed. Markus was nervous at first because Michelle was behind the cameras flicking and flashing.

Michelle preferred to use the cameras she carried and needed nothing from *Porno Magazine's* photo team but their expertise on the lighting equipment. She instructed them on adjusting the panels and lights the way she wished.

She instructed Markus Johnson and Daisy Lace, directing them in all forms of sexual positions, intertwining them, making them do oral suggestive and romantic situations, nearly naked and completely clothed.

During the shoot, they must have changed clothing a dozen times. Then they took a break before they went over to the dojo set and started anew. Markus couldn't keep his eyes off Michelle. She kept sneaking glances at him and occasionally she would give him an outright frown, or stare at him so penetratingly, it made him feel funny. Markus eventually had to look away.

During the break, Michelle made sure she stayed as far away from Markus as possible. Susan ordered a load of Chinese food. The decision was made to eat in the warehouse at a long table. Sparks and Entice were at one end of the table talking. Audra was watching a very disoriented and nervous Markus on the other side of the table. Michelle was not seen. Susan and her photo team were chatting amongst themselves.

They returned to work and spent another four hours doing the photo shoot. It was closely approaching nine in the evening when Sparks rushed everyone who came with him. At seven-thirty in the morning their flight to Japan was leaving, and they still had a few things like packing to do.

Even though he felt awkward around her, Markus didn't want to leave Michelle's presence. He didn't know what to do. His manager felt his emotional state. "Markus," Sparks said waving him over. "I don't know what to tell you, but you gotta do something besides standing over there, looking like an ass."

Markus nodded in agreement but didn't know exactly what to do. Michelle made her move before Markus could think. She walked over to him, a vision of complete mystery and with a raspy voice said. "I dream about flies."

"What?" Markus was surprised she even walked over to him, much less spoke.

"I dream of flies, always have, ever since I was a little girl," she laughed.

"Were you adopted?" He asked.

"What sort of fucking question is that?" She snapped with venom.

"Sorry. I don't know what to say to you."

"You said something strange. You are so strange," Michelle said, packing her cameras. He knew she was about to leave. She probably said something just to see exactly how crazy I am, Markus thought.

"It's been fun, but gotta go," she said then turned around and began walking toward the exit.

"Wait," he yelled.

"What is it?" Michelle asked stopping and turning.

"You dream of flies. Do you dream of two people, a boy being dragged away? Do you dream of people around you saying things, strange things you barely understand? Do you have flashbacks in the middle of the day and faint afterwards?"

"You are crazy. I'm scared of flies. I have always been since I was a little girl, and that is it. I don't know how you knew, but good for you," she laughed at him.

Markus was about to say something else but she said, "I don't know what sort of game you're playing, or what you want from me, but I want nothing from you. I would never mess with or even deal with a person like you. Your profession isn't something I'm into. You disgust me."

She seemed like she was going to rush over and slap him in the face her anger was brewing to such a heated state. It seemed like it was more than Markus being an annoyance with his questions. He didn't want her to leave and didn't want her to think he was crazy. Markus rushed to her before she opened the door, grabbing her arm.

"Get your filthy hands off me!" She yelled.

Her outburst made everyone look. Sparks, Audra, Entice and Susan didn't know what was going on. They saw Markus nervously let go of her arm. "Don't you ever fucking touch me and don't you ever fucking call me again!"

Michelle walked out the warehouse leaving Markus looking stupid, and feeling defeated. He eventually walked over to the others standing shocked to silence. Nothing else was said for awhile until Markus gathered the strength to speak.

"Let's get out of here," he said, shaking his head. "We gotta get up early and catch that flight to Japan."

Entice wanted to say something, but didn't. Audra eyed Markus with curiosity. "At least you did something." Sparks told Markus patting him on the back. "Put all of this in the rearview mirror, my nigga. Tomorrow is a new day. We gotta long flight ahead of us. In Japan we're gonna have the time of our lives. She'll be nothing more than a footnote in our story by the time we get back to these here United States."

Markus knew that was truer than Sparks could ever imagine. Michelle was indeed and would always be a memory, a mysterious portion of his strange and mysterious past.

She walked out the warehouse and reached a hand out for the stair's railing. Michelle stumbled but managed not to fall down the small flight of stairs. Every time she was too close, or whenever she thought of Mr. Excitement, she felt nauseated and faintish. She quickly gathered herself, and ran to where her car was parked. Thinking of how strange the day had gone.

Michelle Watson had been hired to do a photo shoot, and Mr. Excitement was the object she had to photograph. Taking pictures of Mr. Excitement, and Daisy Lace was the worst and most challenging eight hours of her life. She hated the feeling she had when she thought about him, or got close enough to get a good look at him.

She wasn't sure why he knew that she was adopted, and about the flies. Michelle had to get Mr. Excitement out of her mind, her life was never dull, and she had problems of her own. She scrambled inside a pocket for the keys to her car, opened the door, hopped inside her car and slammed the door shut. Before she could put the key into the ignition, Michelle had to open the door again. Everything she had for lunch spewed out of her in one big rush on the side of the street. Michelle felt woozy. She slammed the door and drove off.

"What the fuck is wrong with me?" her breath was weak.

"Why do you make me feel like this?"

Thoughts of Mr. Excitement plagued her. Inside her mind a swarm of flies buzzed and fluttered around with his image as their faces.

34

The flight to Tokyo was twelve hours and thirty minutes long. Sparks took a PSP video game system. He had a dozen games and movies. Audra took her iPod and a novel. Markus carried an iPod. He was also laden with thoughts of Michelle, heavy on his mind. They were flying first class courtesy of Smut Central. Vonchell had a seat next to Markus. She, Daisy Lace and about eight others associated with Smut Central Entertainment were on the same flight. Markus made a stewardess keep the alcohol coming. He fell into a drunken slumber.

Markus was roused awake in the middle of the flight by Vonchell unzipping his jeans. She put a hand inside his pants and started manipulating his dick before he could say anything. Her hands were very experienced, her fingers long and talented. She stroked his dick. He allowed it for a couple of beats before he said, "Get your hands off my dick."

"Let's go in the bathroom and join the mile high club," Vonchell purred with sex on her mind.

"No." he said. He reached inside his pants and aggressively removed Vonchell's hand. "I'm gonna fuck you good for the filming, and that's about it."

"Suit yourself," she said nonchalantly, "If that's how I get your dick then so be it."

She looked over at the adjacent row of seats to someone from Smut Central and saw Meeko Delight, an Asian American porn actress. She along with Vonchell and Markus were starring in *Black Geisha*.

"I'll get my wings with or without you," Vonchell said to him. "Heterosexual or lesbian, it matters little."

"Go ahead, you got my permission. Do you. If you get my meaning…?"

He put headphones into his ears, closed his eyes and began listening to music. Moments passed. Once again Markus felt some delicate hand inside his pants. He grabbed the wrist, was about to squeeze it as hard as he could. Markus opened his eyes and was surprised to see the petite and alluring, slanted eyed Meeko Delight.

"Let's get some practice, Mr. Excitement," Meeko said with a touch of an accent.

Markus eyed the lovely Asian, and smiled. He was instantly aroused by her eyes alone. They were narrow and deeply filled with sexual lust. Green like jade, her eyes twinkled like jewels. He never worked with her but had seen a few of her movies. She was a porn superstar. She had never been with a black man in a film as far as he knew. She was a part of this exclusive porn division, introduced to him by his agent, Audra, and Smut Central Entertainment. He was officially down with the big league.

Markus felt the urge of sex upon him. He assumed it was more from his sexual programming than anything else. He only wanted to have sex in a professional situation, and had thoughts of Michelle rewinding in the brain. Meeko guided Markus to the bathroom. They entered and she locked the door behind them.

"Practice…?" Markus hissed.

Meeko Delight was a lithe and petite, Oriental treat. Standing at a small five feet two inches, with very strong legs and feet no larger than a four, she wore a simple dress with Oriental calligraphy print and a thin loose fitting sweater.

Markus propped her small body on top of the sink and slipped a hand up her dress. There wasn't anything under the dress. He imagined Vonchell had already been in the dress and had eaten Meeko's panties. He laughed at the thought. Meeko was really wet.

Professionally his finger moved her clitoris around in a circular motion then he parted her vaginal lips. Meeko let out a low sounding moan. Reaching over, she undid his belt and felt inside his boxer shorts.

She let out a loud sigh, "Oh my God! Vonchell wasn't lying."

Meeko's slanted eyes closed as tightly as they could. Markus had moved her hands off of his penis and javelined it inside her. Her nails dug deeply into his shoulders. Meeko held on for dear life as he initiated the first thrust, then the second came, then the third. Meeko began screaming wildly at the top of her lungs.

"You should have never mentioned her," he said to Meeko, putting a hand over her mouth.

Meeko was very tight and Markus's dick was very big with both length and girth. If Markus hadn't pushed inside her so aggressively he might not have gotten it in. He loved Chinese food and wanted to eat Meeko out to loosen her up but she mentioned Vonchell and that aroused something a bit more animalistic in him.

He rammed his dick inside Meeko hard. Her legs instantly lost their strength and began dangling down on the side of the sink. Markus let go of her mouth long enough to grab both of her ankles, her slippers fell to the bathroom floor. He hoisted her legs on his shoulders and completely lifted her off the sink. He began pumping his dick inside her.

"No! You're in too much," Meeko yelled before he put his hand over her mouth again, muffling her screaming.

He wasn't sure if she was enjoying it or not. He simply concentrated on Vonchell's image, Meeko's tight little pussy, and fucking. He fucked her hard for about twenty minutes. Then he let go of her mouth with one hand and switched arms.

Meeko was suspended in the air one moment with nothing but his penetrating dick in her, keeping her from hitting the floor. Then gravity kicked in and she fell.

Markus wasn't quite finished with Meeko. His dick burst with his orgasm. Shooting a load on Meeko's face, Markus watched her fall to the floor, breathing heavily, and moaning in pain.

Markus was still jerking his dick with long strokes, aiming all of the semen that gushed out of him in spurts. Never the sort of woman who enjoyed nuts in her face, Meeko tried her best to dodge the hosing. Markus put a foot on Meeko's forehead so she couldn't get away. He held Meeko's frightened, face steady, and she got a face full of sperm.

Meeko was whimpering when Markus pulled up his jeans, buckled his belt and walked out the bathroom. She decided once she wiped her face off and walked out the bathroom that she would never mention Vonchell to Mr. Excitement again. Meeko had to walk past Markus to get to her seat. He saw her limping with a hand on one of her hips.

"I like it rough," Meeko said, smiling at him before she sat.

"Next time I'll be rough then," Markus said to Meeko Delight while looking at Vonchell.

When the plane landed at Haneda Airport in Ota, Tokyo Japan, and they had retrieved their luggage, they were greeted by a lovely looking Japanese woman outside the main entrance. She stood in front of a limo holding a sign that read, *Welcome SCE, Mr. Excitement, Vonchell and Daisy Lace*. Emiho was her name and Markus figured she was the welcome wagon. Sparks thought the woman said, "I'm a hoe." So when she said her name he said. "I'm a hoe as well. We should hook up."

Meeko broke out in gleeful laughter and explained things to the rest of them. Everyone with the exception of Sparks laughed.

"What?" he asked glancing at everyone. "She looks just like one."

Emiho was a professional woman who was hired to be the guide while they were in Japan. They had a long and strenuous nearly half a year ahead of them. They were also jet lagged and tired. They all wanted to get to the hotel and to sleep.

Markus was all eyes once the limo drove off. Tokyo city was presented to Markus, to all of them. There was much to see and things were just getting started. Markus did not even glance at the *Black Geisha* script during the flight. But he took a look at it while they were on their way to the heart of Tokyo City and the exquisite five star accommodations of Hotel Nikko Tokyo.

Tee-Neck obviously wasn't worried about expenses. Markus

decided to forget about Vonchell, and forget about everything else that was bothering him. He was going to get acquainted with the script and the city and enjoy the experience.

    Entice had been left with Sparks's vehicle and the keys to the five bedroom mansion until Markus, Sparks, Audra and the rest of the SCE gang returned. Entice wasn't sure what sort of future the porno industry held for her. It didn't matter in any particular way as far as she was concerned. She was concerned with very little.

    Feeling jealous of the rest of them, Entice wished she could have gone. Japan was such an exotic place. She was sure it was going to be a crazy experience for Markus and Sparks. It was a place she always wanted to visit.

    Cali was in a van trailing behind Sparks's car. He had been following Markus, Sparks and Entice around ever since Markus left Gwyneth's penthouse apartment the last time he went.

    Since that Friday Markus picked up his daughter and drove to New Jersey, Cali was incensed in getting even with Markus and Sparks. The goons who were with Cali the day they ambushed him at Jingling Babes were in the van along with a few other thugs.

    "I wonder where they going?" One of Cali's cronies asked him while they were at the airport.

    "Who gives a fuck? I don't." Cali snapped. "They took a plane but they'll be back. That bitch didn't go with them," he said, pointing out the window. "Look, she's getting back in the car. We are gonna make an example out of her."

    "Yeah, I can't wait. That bitch was waving a knife in my face after they taped me to the chair," one of Cali's cronies said, while driving the van.

"Wherever she's going, we following," Cali told whoever, looking back at his squad of goons in the back of the van.

He gave them the most evil smile he could muster. A smile minus a couple of front teeth, compliments of the beat down Markus had given him.

"Once we get our hands on her. You guys go ahead and have your way with the bitch. Make sure you beat the shit out of her afterwards! Then kill the fucking bitch and toss her in a ditch," Cali laughed. "I want her dead."

35

Entice had dropped Markus and Sparks off at the airport. She drove back to the mansion in Jersey. Now she had the whole house to herself, and didn't know what to do. Tee-Neck said he had some sort of work lined up for her in the coming weeks. Entice was supposed to be doing a couple of girl on girl scenes, and a film where she had to fuck two white dudes.

Things didn't seem the way they did when she first got in the porn game. Entice was nervous about things. Vonchell introduced her to the porn industry. She didn't like Vonchell much.

Vonchell used to work at the club Entice danced at. Vonchell was making way more money because men seemed to be drawn to her. When Vonchell suggested they do some extracurricular activities that would make them more money, Entice went along with the idea.

Vonchell introduced Entice to Tee-Neck, Smut Central Entertainment and the adult entertainment biz. Thus she had introduced Entice to Mr. Excitement. Entice was a loner, she hardly had any friends and fewer family. Markus and Sparks were beginning to become her family, if they knew it or not.

She walked inside the mansion with hardly any care. She didn't pay attention to the black van that sped past her on the highway. She wasn't in Queensbridge; she was in a gated community on the hills. Cali knew she was going to Jersey when she drove to the Holland Tunnel. They knew where Markus Johnson had relocated.

"Let's drive ahead of her and get the drop on her," he said to the driver.

"Okay," he said. "Are we gonna break in?"

"Nah," Cali answered. "The place might have a burglar alarm. There are a lot of big shrubs in the front. We can hide behind them and jump out on her before she closes the door. That's exactly how it's gonna go down."

As soon as Entice opened the door and attempted to close it, a foot prevented the closing. There was no time for a scream. The door burst open and six men pushed themselves in.

Before she could say anything someone punched her in the face. Everything around her turned upside down. She was in the worst of pain, felt blood tricking down her nose. She fell to the floor then got hit again. Entice knew nothing else.

She was roused out of unconsciousness, not knowing how long she had been out. Her eyes fluttered open and she realized someone was on top of her. Entice tried to scream, but a sock had been stuffed inside her mouth.

"Yeah bitch!" She heard one of them say. "Remember me, huh? The one you and your friends taped to the chair…?"

Entice was naked on a bed, in one of the bedrooms, her wrists bound to the bedposts. The guy on top of her was forcing himself inside. She tried to kick her legs out wildly, but couldn't. Other men were in the room. Two tightly held her legs and had her spread eagle.

This wasn't the first time she'd been raped. The others had taken their turn while she was still unconscious. Entice felt the soreness in her vagina and her ass. She was painfully aware that a couple of them had taken her roughly in the anus. The one they taped to the chair in Jingling Babes was fucking her then ejaculated inside her. She tried screaming loudly as she could, but not so much as a peep could be heard.

After he was finished, another took his turn, and then another. Entice wasn't sure how long the raping had been going on. She stopped feeling pain and began feeling sick and nauseous. They were coming in her. Entice never felt so violated, disrespected, and hurt. She wished they would kill her, and get it over with.

She threw up everything she had for breakfast, but it had no where to go but back down her throat, thanks to the sock stuffed inside her mouth. She kept choking and suffocating. She stopped breathing with one of the goon's dick still inside her. She was dead and he was on top, riding her corpse...

Cali watched from the van as his cronies rushed the house. He gave them time to do their dirt then he would make his grand entrance. Cali waited in the van for twenty minutes. He felt that was more than enough time for them to terrorize her. Before he stepped out of the van his cell phone rang.

"What you want, Tanisha?" he said, sounding annoyed.

"Please," she begged. "Don't…"

"Don't what?" He cut her off. "Don't what? Don't hurt your little friend. Bitch, did you see what they did to me," he said, looking into the rearview mirror and cracking a smile.

Cali saw where he was missing a couple of teeth. He frowned then hung up, hopped out of the van, and cautiously walked inside the huge house. The furniture looked expensive. Markus Johnson was doing better than he imagined. He heard commotion coming from upstairs and went in that direction. They were in one of the rooms. He wondered why they dragged the bitch up the stairs.

"Why didn't you niggas beat her up, down here…?" They didn't have to answer him. He knew why they dragged her upstairs when she entered the room. He saw them raping Entice.

Cali watched them in shock and disgust. They were doing exactly what he told them to do. He didn't want things to go the way they were. He was just saying shit, popping shit. He didn't intend for them to rape the girl, at least not literally. He didn't know his boys were as nasty and ruthless as this. Cali wasn't the sort of dude who would rape a woman. He wondered why they didn't use condoms.

"You niggas are nasty." Cali told them. "Have you ever heard of DNA? You're leaving a whole lot of evidence inside her."

Cali's own words made him laugh. He was more disgusted by what he was watching than humored in spite of laughing. He didn't know what else to do. She was going to be smacked around. Cali figured no one would care about a black porno bitch. The only ones who would care were Markus and Sparks. Now he wasn't certain about things. His goons had nut in her. That was DNA and it spelled evidence. Now they had to get rid of her. Everything he said during the thrill of the chase, and out of anger had been realized. He wasn't amused by what was going on. He had finally seen enough,

"Get off of her!" He ordered the guy fucking Entice.

Entice's body jerked and jolted. She almost broke through the ropes tied to the bedposts her spasm was so violent. Piss and shit flowed out of her. The guy inside her jumped off as soon as he felt the hot piss gushing out her vagina.

"Nasty R-Kelly bitch," he yelled before he smacked her in the face.

The others laughed while Cali looked at them and shook his head. Things weren't going the way he intended. It was like he was looking at his cronies for the very first time. They were horrible monsters. Cali was the leader of the monsters.

The guy grabbed a bed sheet and used that to wipe himself. Cali watched everything. They were a bit too obedient. He wanted revenge, but that was all. He didn't want the girl messed up like that. Cali scrunched up his face.

"Nigga, you went inside a woman who had about six nuts inside her, and you got the nerve to be scared of piss?"

Entice's body jerked one more time then her body went deathly limp. The guys holding her legs let them fall. Her legs had no life in them. She was dead. Cali cautiously took the soaked sock out of her mouth. He reeled back. Her breath smelled worse than shit.

"She isn't breathing." Cali announced.

Entice choked to death on her own vomit. Green stuff began leaking out of a mouth. Her eyes were wide open in terror and shock. They were eyes Cali would remember for the rest of his life. They were looking directly at him. He slowly backed away from the bed, from the corpse, from his cronies.

"She's dead," he said to himself.

"We were gonna kill her anyway," one of his goons said,

pulling his pants up.

"Shut the fuck up!" Cali snapped. "All o' you are nasty murdering fucks!"

Cali walked out the room, out of the house and went to the van. His cronies followed.

Inside the van he snapped, "Everybody lay low. None of this happened. You guys put evidence in her. I ain't touch that bitch. Think about that before you open your mouths and start talking or snitching," he said, watching all their expressions changing.

Cali smiled but he was feeling so foul inside. They had killed a bitch. There was really nothing to smile about.

"We did what you told us to," the driver said.

"Nigga, please just drive!" Cali snapped.

He was disgusted but scared as hell. There was more than fear brewing inside him. Somewhere there was sadness and pity for the bitch they raped and murdered. Cali was glad he didn't so much as touch her. Whoever walks into the house is going to get the shock of their life, Cali thought. With any luck it would be Markus Johnson.

He wasn't sure if leaving the girl's body in the house was the right thing to do. They should have wrapped the body up in something, dug the deepest hole they could dig and buried the evidence. Maybe they should have doused the corpse with gasoline and burned the whole damn house down.

It didn't matter.

They were in the van and on there way back to Brooklyn. The plan was to act like nothing happened. Cali figured he would be in the clear if anything came of it. He was the only one who walked in the house with shoes. He planned on getting rid of them as soon as he got the chance. He was the only one wearing gloves and he was the only one who hadn't touched the girl much less raped her or ejaculated in her. In spite of everything, he laughed.

"I hope you at least liked the bitch," Cali said to a Markus who wasn't around, laughing.

He didn't know what sort of relationship Markus and Sparks had with the dead girl. He should have probed Tanisha for more info, but she always changed the subject when the subject was Markus Johnson.

All he knew was the bitch was with Markus and Sparks when they ambushed him at the club. She was with them all the time. As far as he was concerned she was as responsible for his missing teeth as Markus and Sparks. She had just paid for her mistake- for their mistake. Don't ever fuck with Cali.

HOMICIDE
CENTRAL

Prologue
The Past

It was way past midnight, very cold and windy. A black stray cat walked by. That was bad luck from where he stood. Regardless of how smoothly the pick ups and drop offs were, they still made James more nervous when something spooky happened. He tapped his last cigarette out the box. The box fell to the floor and landed beside the four stubs he had smoked back to back. He rummaged inside a pocket for a lighter. He flicked it and flicked it, no flame. He became aggravated and tossed the lighter.

"Fuck!" he exclaimed. "What is taking them so long?"

He was in the back of the clinic. This was the second time he picked a baby up here. He had never done a pick up in the same place twice. He didn't like the way things were going on this one. The money was good. All he cared about was getting paid. He didn't know where the babies went once he dropped them off at the airport. All he knew was the shit was illegal. He was a criminal. What the fuck did he care? What was one crime from another? James wasn't the philosophical sort. The door to the service entrance cracked open. Good, he thought with nervousness. He was so damn nervous. He wanted to get things done and over with. He saw a man stick his face out the crack of the door.

"Over here," James whispered to the guy. "I'm over here."

"Oh," the man said once he walked completely out and into the cold.

The alley was dark and the streets dismally empty. He always took the newborns and vanished. Things went smooth. He had nothing to worry about.

"Over here," James said again.

He took a step closer. "Here they are," the man said to James.

He was holding a bigger bundle then James expected. No, James thought. The guy was holding two bundles. James arched an eyebrow.

"What do you mean, they?" He asked.

"She had twins," the man answered.

"What?" James exclaimed louder than he wanted. "Twins…?" He cursed under his breath. "No one told me anything about twins."

"We didn't know," the man said nervously.

James took another step and got a closer look. There were two bundles, two newborns wrapped up. He didn't know what to do.

"Don't we get more money?" the guy questioned. "I mean, there are two. Don't we get double?"

James had a bag full of money. They already paid the dude half. He reached into his jacket and pulled out the other part of the payment.

"Double?" He said. "All I got is this." He showed the guy the bag. "No one said anything about twins."

James was never in this sort of situation before. He decided to make it short and sour. "You should have said something."

"What are we gonna do?" the guy asked.

James knew the guy was a low life. Any person who would sell their children was the lowest of the low. He figured he was as low if not lower. He was the transporter. He wasn't sure about what was going down. He knew he was apart of something that went far beyond smuggling babies out the country. He was smart enough to not want to know more. He was smart enough to do what he was paid to do.

"I don't know." James told him.

He gave the guy a keener look within the darkness of the alley and moved closer. One lamp post gave of the dimmest luminance. Even with that he knew the guy holding the bundled up newborns was some sort of addict, perhaps cocaine, perhaps heroin. It were either or. And most of them were Black though James had gotten a white baby once and a few Latino babies.

"I think we should get more money. She had twins..."

The guy started ranting about it. He started hugging the babies closer. James wasn't sure if it was because of the cold. The guy looked like he wasn't going to give the babies up.

"I don't know how much they paid you already. I don't know how much is inside this bag either. All I know is that I gotta deadline. I was sent here to get a baby." He tossed the bag of money at the guy's feet. "Just give me one. I don't give a fuck."

"But," the guy stuttered. "She had twins. It's gonna be documented like she lost the babies but she had twins."

James moved closer. The guy looked like he was going to run inside the clinic. "Easy," he whispered. "Relax. Let me think things through."

James knew everything was done secret. The clinic was run by people who were down with whatever was going on, the doctors who delivered the baby and the nurses, everyone was down. Everyone was getting paid like he was.

The guy was having mixed feelings. It was more than the twins and the money. The guy was selling his children. The guy was a low life but he was having second thoughts. James wasn't sure about anything. He didn't know what to do. No. James knew. The guy wanted more money.

That was the size of things, that and nothing more. There was no turning back. No renegotiating and no double dealing. The guy was business. James never took business personal, never asked and did what he had to do.

"I don't know about this," James told him with finality. "I don't have a number to call. All I know is the money is on the ground, in that bag." He nudged his jaw at the bag. "Take the money. Give me one of the babies or both, I don't give a fuck. I would think they pay you more than enough."

"No," the guy said in defiance.

James saw his hand reach for the doorknob. He cursed out in frustration. He never got into any sort of situation before during a job. He knew what he was supposed to do if something like this happened. They told him exactly what to do. They hired James because he was the sort of person capable of doing what had to be done.

"Ok," James said with the calmest voice he could muster.

He was nervous, very nervous. Nervousness however never hindered him. It only made him keener. "Let me call somebody. Maybe we can get you more money." He reached into a pocket. There was a cell phone in his jacket, a cell phone and something else. "Take the money." He laughed. "It's so windy. We wouldn't want the bag of money to blow away."

The guy nodded his head in approval. James watched him stoop down. He was holding both bundled babies in one arm. They were as silent as the night. All that could be heard was the wind whistling in the back of the alley. James gave the area a stronger look. He was quite sure no one was around. Instead of pulling out the cell phone he pulled out the other thing inside his pocket. The pistol had a silencer on the tip of it. His employer told him to kill and take the baby if the person proposed a problem. The guy was definitely proposing a problem. But there were babies. She had twins.

He pulled the trigger. The gun fired off with a soft sucking sound. The bullet went between his eyes and out the top of his head. James cursed when the man fell. The babies hit the ground with him and tumbled. He heard the babies cry out. They were newborn babies. He shot the guy in the head again for good measure. He moved closer.

He was a professional. He knew it wasn't the time to be slow. He picked up the babies. The twins were wrapped tight. He wasn't sure if they were hurt or if they were cold. He couldn't even see their faces. They were crying. They were alive. James grabbed the bag of money. It didn't make any sense to leave it. What could the guy do with the payment now? He shot the guy in the head a third time. He had to make sure he was dead. He figured three bullets in the face were enough to kill anyone.

"Fuck!" James exclaimed to the corpse. "You shouldn't have given me problems. You should have taken the money."

James tucked the bag of money back in his jacket. He was wearing gloves. The gun and the silencer were ambiguous; the serial numbers were scratched off. No one would find out anything. He dropped the gun. He rushed out of the alley. His car was parked on the street. The headlights were out but the engine was running. He looked around. The area was still desolate. He grinned. James had nothing to worry about. The babies had already simmered down.

He popped the trunk and put the babies in the special compartment. There was room for two. James thanked whoever for that. If there wasn't room for both he would have had to leave one of them on the street. He wasn't sure how he would have felt if he had done that. He had some scruples not many but even James Peterson had his limits. He figured leaving a newborn on the street was something that would get you a ticket straight to hell.

He wasn't sure what sort of ticket he would get for what he was doing. What he did know was the person who hired him, his employer, whoever that was. That person was going to go as low as hell was. He was going to be all the way in hell's boiler room.

The present

James spied on the young lady for weeks. He knew all about her. She was some sort of freelance photographer who lived in the East Village. Her occupation made him laugh. He knew what she was designed for. She was designed to be a sex slave. She was designed to be the perfect whore.

He thought two decades back. It was so strange. He had vague memories of each and every pick up he had done and each and every baby he abducted looked no different from one another, if he got a look at them at all. This woman, Michelle Watson was one of the twins. It was the reason why he remembered her so well. The twins were the first assignment that proposed a problem. It was the first time he had to kill a person on the job.

Now he was a killer. Now he kills the babies but the babies are all grown up. In a sense James was their first and their last experience. He was their Alpha and their Omega. He was no longer a courier but it was the same thing. He was still involved in Randleman and now his involvement cycled a complete three hundred and sixty degrees. He still saw the Randleman product as babies since he had been around when they were born. He had for the past two decades snatched these babies up and now they were grown and intergraded into society. Most of them were integrated in a big way. Most were celebrities or high profile socialites.

It was only fitting for James to be there when their lives ended. Sometimes the Randleman Protocol wore off. Additional hypnosis lessens the effects of the original programming. Some of the kids have multiple programming. Sometimes a person would pre order the product and then have a change of mind. Then someone else would want that same product but with a different sort of programming. He didn't know too much about anything. He just did what he was told. He wasn't sure who was worse, the people purchasing or his employer, the seller.

It was all crazy, scientific and mystical bullshit dealing with flies and things that dated back to ancient Egypt. Why things went wrong mattered little. What did matter was things had to be rectified. Murder was the best way to rectify things. So many people's lives would be ruined if the world started putting two and two together. There were so many influential people involved in the Randleman Project, politicians, business tycoons, diplomats and 'A' list celebrities.

James was fifty years old. He killed more than a dozen people in his life; men, women and children. Michelle Watson was another assignment and nothing more. She was going to be an easy kill. She wasn't a socialite and she wasn't famous. She hadn't risen to some sort of celebrity status like the others. She hadn't any bodyguards. She wasn't in the spotlight. For some reason most of the children who were abducted and underwent the hypnosis grew up being superstars, that or high class whores. James wondered why it was always one or the other. His wondering was brief. He didn't care enough to ponder it for any real length. He knew caring and being curious about things would only get him killed.

He had to be emotionless. He never cared about anything but money. His employer paid him handsomely, had been paying him generously for the past three decades. He knew they liked him because he cared so little. His employer appreciated that he never talked. James did whatever he was told and said nothing.

It was close to the stroke of midnight and drizzling. He sat in his car. James was parked across the street from the building she resided in. Every night for the past couple of days she came home at roughly the same time. Normally her working situation was erratic. The last couple of days were the most consistent. He figured she had some sort of photo assignment that lasted a couple of days or she landed a steadier job. Either way, he analyzed the doorman schedule and knew tonight was a good night to kill Michelle Watson.

There was a fifteen minute gap between the doormen's shift. Every night at midnight one door man would leave and the other would arrive and for the last couple of days Michelle had gotten home during the gap between the shifts. The building had no video cameras. That was the best part. If the building had some sort of surveillance it wouldn't have hindered him but he liked for things to go smoothly and appreciated the fact that there weren't any cameras. Things were going to go smoothly.

Two days ago James snuck into the building during the gap in the shifts. He knew exactly which apartment Michelle lived in.

He went to the door and jimmied the lock open. It only took him two minutes. It took him three minutes to get inside the building, reach her door and walk back out the building again. While he was leaving he walked by Michelle. She walked into the building. She didn't give him a second glance. He was so close to her he got a whiff of the perfume she was wearing. He got a good look at her face from the corner of an eye. She was the most beautiful women he had ever seen. Most of them were.

If they grew up anything less than drop dead gorgeous, they were exterminated. He didn't know much about things but he did know that. He knew most of the children abducted never fit the criteria and were disposed of. He wasn't certain of the criteria but he knew it had something to do with the children's genetics and their looks. One baby looked exactly like another to him. And he didn't know shit about genetics. His employer assured him there were ways of determining whether or not a child would grow up to be gorgeous or not. Michelle Watson was drop dead gorgeous. Soon she would just be drop dead.

Michelle was so tired. She recently acquired a steady photo shooting gig for a very popular hip-hop magazine. Nothing in her life was ever steady before. A nine to five wasn't something she was used to. She walked in her apartment building, yawned then waved at the doorman. The afternoon doorman yawned and waved back. They hadn't switched shifts yet. It wasn't the older man at the door. It was the young one, the cute one. Michelle said, "Hey sexy doorman," And went to her mailbox.

She knew the cute doorman was looking at her butt and admiring her body, like every man on the planet did. She wanted to turn around and flirt with him but she was too tired. The doorman was a black man. Most black men made Michelle think of Markus Johnson. If her mind wandered towards thoughts of him, she knew she would throw-up or worse, blackout. She didn't want to do neither.

She retrieved her mail, it was mostly bills. She was waiting for a letter that didn't seem like it would ever arrive. She frowned and slammed the mailbox door before she locked it. Michelle went to the staircase and jogged up two flights and then jogged to her door. She immediately felt something was wrong as soon as she walked inside and locked the door. Her dog didn't greet her.

"Randleman," she uttered, "Randleman, where are you?"

"Funny, that you would name your dog Randleman. I had to muzzle him and put him in a pillow case. He's a feisty little terrier. I haven't harmed him." Michelle heard a man's voice say. She panicked.

Her first instinct was to back herself to the door. It was dark inside the apartment. She knew she clicked on the night light before she left that morning. The guy shut off the night light. How long has he been in my apartment, she thought? What does he want with me?

"I have a gun," she lied.

"No, you don't," the man said. "I mean you no harm."

"Fuck you!" She snapped.

She knew the man was creeping up behind her. She turned and swung a kick. Her assailant wasn't expecting that. Her kick was professional and powerful. Her foot smacked him on the side of the face. It sent him reeling back. He staggered into the living room and got knocked over some furniture. Before he could rise she jumped over the love seat and was all over him, stomping and kicking him in the face. All her strikes were direct and precise. He could do nothing but cover his face with his arms.

"I'm here to help…" She heard him say while she was kicking

and stomping. "Stop it…"

"Fuck you!" She yelled.

They heard the lock on the door click. Michelle looked over at the door. She wasn't sure what was going on. She backed away from her assailant. Her assailant staggered to his feet. She didn't know what was going on.

"What is going on?" she asked.

It was almost comical. Here she was in her living room with a stranger whom just attacked her. Now they were standing together peering at her front door in the darkness. Someone was picking the locks, they both knew. Her assailant looked as nervous as she was.

"What is going on?" She asked a second time, this time in whisper.

"I wanted to say, come with me if you want to live when you walked in," he told her.

"*The Terminator* movie," she uttered. "Is someone trying to kill me?"

"Yeah," the guy nodded. He went into a pocket and withdrew a small revolver. "My name is Gary Zimmerman. I'm a private investigator. I mean you no harm. The person trying to get into your apartment does."

"Huh?"

Michelle didn't know what to think. She wanted to say something but nothing came out her mouth.

"The person picking your lock is a professional killer. He was hired to murder you and Markus Johnson."

Michelle heard Gary Zimmerman say Markus's name. She fainted.

"Shit." Gary blurted.

He chastised himself for saying Markus's name. He didn't

surmise Michelle Watson having similar symptoms as Markus. Actually he figured Michelle to be a successful Randleman specimen. Markus had undergone an additional hypnotic procedure. Did she get reprogrammed as well? He wasn't sure. What he was sure of was James Peterson.

He finished jimmying the lock. The door swung open. James figured the commotion inside the house would mask the little noise he made when he picked the lock. Michelle had gotten home ten minutes early. That and James knew an intruder was in her apartment. In any event, he wasn't about to abort the mission. He had to know who the intruder was whether he got the chance to kill Michelle or not.

They were staring at each other, face to face.

"Who are you?" James asked Gary.

"Funny you would ask that, James. The people you've been killing usually want to know who they are."

"You know too much," James worded.

"It's a sickness."

"People die from sicknesses," James sneered in the dark.

There was a gun pointed at him. He wasn't sure how proficient the guy was with firearms but he was holding one properly. He was holding it like a police officer. James had a gun of his own and it had a silencer on the tip of it. He wasn't sure if he could raise his hand fast enough. He didn't want to underestimate a person who could follow him around. He dared not underestimate a person who knew as much as this person did.

"What now?" He asked.

"I don't know. You leave I guess. No one is going to harm Michelle as long as I live."

"I guess we are going to have to make sure you die soon," James laughed.

He slowly backed out the apartment and closed the door. Gary was so damn nervous. He was sweating everywhere. James had eyes like a snake, cold blooded eyes. He was a husky man. Gary wasn't certain if he could have put him down with one bullet. He wanted to check on Michelle. He didn't. He ran to the dining room and grabbed a chair. He locked the front door and put the chair up under the doorknob. Then he ran to a window that showed the front of the building. James Peterson was casually walking back to his car. He didn't glance up at the apartment. He was way too cool, calm, and deadly.

To the Dream Team:
Special thank you to the Augustus Mnuscript Team: Jason Claiborne, Tamiko Maldonado, Juliet White and Anthony Whyte. Another great job done.

WHERE
HIP-HOP
LITERATURE
BEGINS...

AUGUSTUS
PUBLISHING

Augustus Publishing was created to unify minds with entertaining, hard-hitting tales from a hood near you. Hip Hop literature interprets contemporary times and connects to readers through shared language, culture and artistic expression. From street tales and erotica to coming-of age sagas, our stories are endearing, filled with drama, imagination and laced with a Hip Hop steez

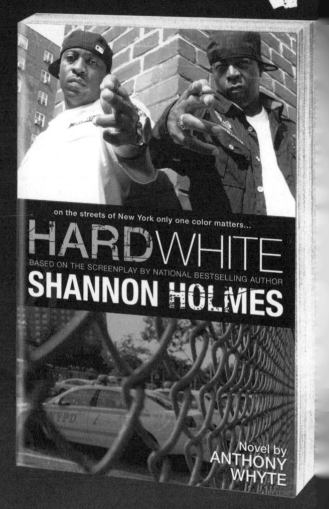

on the streets of New York only one color matters...

HARD WHITE

BASED ON THE SCREENPLAY BY NATIONAL BESTSELLING AUTHOR

SHANNON HOLMES

Novel by
ANTHONY
WHYTE

Hard White: On the street of New York only on color matters
Novel By Anthony Whyte Based on the screenplay by Shannon Holmes

The streets are pitch black...A different shade of darkness has drifted to the North Bro
hood known as Edenwald. Sleepless nights, there is no escaping dishonesty, disrespe
ignorance, hostility, treachery, violence, karma... Hard White metered out to the resider
quan and Precious have big dreams but must overcome much in order to manifest their
the novel is a story of triumph and tribulations of two people's journey to make it des
Nail biting drama you won't ever forget...Once you pick it up you can't put it down. De
Anthony Whyte based on the screenplay by Shannon Holmes, the story comes at you
offering an insight to what it takes to get off the streets. It shows a woman's unWlimite
man. Precious is a rider and will do it all again for her man, Melquan... His love for th
be bloodily severed. Her love for him will melt the coldest heart...Together their lives
ously over the crucible of Hard White. Read the novel and see why they make the n

When Love Turns To Hate
By Sharron Doylee

regulating from down south. He rides with a new ruthless partner, and they'r
money. The partners mercilessly go after a shady associate who is caught in an
s their road to riches. Petie and his two sons have grown apart. Renee, their m
decision when one of her sons wild-out. Desperately, she tries to keep her w
ile holding onto what's left of her family. Venus fights for life after suffering a br
are goes to great lengths to make sure her best friend's attacker stays ruine
aining and teeming with betrayal, corruption, and murder,   When Lo
ixed with romance gone awry. The drama will leave you panting fo

NATIONAL BESTSELLING AUTHOR

ANTHONY WHYTE

STREET CHIĆ

A NOVEL

Street Chic
By Anthony Whyte

...se comes across the desk of detective Sheryl Street, from the Dade county larce...
...ursuing the investigation she discovers that it threatens to unfold some details of...
...was left buried in the Washington Heights area of New York City. Her duties as de...
...nst a family that had emotionally destabilized her. Street ran away from a world s...
...to do with. The murder of a friend brings her back as law and order. Surely as night ti...
...Street's forced into a resolve she cannot walk away from. Loyalty is tested when a de...
...made. When you read this dark and twisted novel you'll find out if allegiance to her...
...er. A most interesting moral conundrum exists in the dramatic tension that is S...

SMUT central
By Brandon McCalla

Markus Johnson, so mysterious he barely knows who he is. An infant left at the doorstep of an orphanage. After fleeing his refuge, he was taken in by a couple with a perverse appetite for sexual indiscretions, only to become a star in the porn industry... Dr. Nancy Adler, a shrink who gained a peculiar patient, unlike any she has ever encountered. A young African American man who faints upon sight of a woman he has never met, having flashbacks of a past he never knew existed. A past that contradicts the few things he knows about himself... Sex and lust tangled in a web so disgustingly tantalizing and demented. Something evil, something demonic... Something beyond the far reaches of a porn stars mind, peculiar to a well established shrink, leaving an old NYPD detective on the verge of solving a case that has been a dead end for years... all triggered by desires for a mysterious woman...

$14.95 / / 9780982541586

Dead And Stinkin'
By Stephen Hewett

Stephen Hewett Collection brings you love as crime. Timeless folklores of adventure, heroes and heroines suffering for love. Can deep unconditional love overcome any obstacles? What is ghetto love? One time loyal friends turned merciless enemies. Humorous and powerful Dead and Stinkin' is tragic and twisted folktales from author Stephen Hewett. The Stephen Hewett Collection comes alive with 3 intensely gripping short stories of undying love, coupled with modern day lies, deceit and treachery.

$14.95 / / 9780982541555

Power of the P
By James Hendricks

Erotica at its gritty best, Power of the P is the seductive story of an entrepreneur who wields his powerful status in unimaginable — and sometimes unethical — ways. This exotic ride through the underworld of sex and prostitution in the hood explores how sex is leveraged to gain advantage over friends and rivals alike, and how sometimes the white collar world and the streets aren't as different as we thought they were.

$14.95 // 9780982541579

America's Soul
By Erick S Gray

Soul has just finished his 18-month sentence for a parole violation. Still in love with his son's mother, America, he wants nothing more than for them to become a family and move on from his past. But while Soul was in prison, America's music career started blowing up and she became entangled in a rocky relationship with a new man, Kendall. Kendall is determined to keep his woman by his side, and America finds herself caught in a tug of war between the two men. Soul turns his attention to battling the street life that landed him in jail — setting up a drug program to rid the community of its tortuous meth problem — but will Soul's efforts cross his former best friend, the murderous drug kingpin Omega?

$14.95 // 9780982541548

The lights went out
and the
mayhem began.

It's gritty in the city but hotter in Brooklyn where a small community in east Flatbush must come to grips with its greatest threat, self-destruction. August 14 and 15, 2003, the eastern section of the United States is crippled by a major shortage of electrical power, the worst in US history. Blackout, the spellbinding novel is based on the epic motion picture, directed by Jerry Lamothe. A thoroughly riveting story with delectable details of families caught in a harsh 48 hours of random violent acts, exploding in deadly conflict. There's a message in everything… even the bullet. The author vividly places characters on the stage of life and like pieces on a chess-board, expertly moves them to a tumultuous end. Voila! Checkmate, a literary triumph. Blackout is a masterpiece. This heart-stopping, page-turning drama is moving fast. Blackout is destined to become an American classic.

BASED ON SCREENPLAY BY **JERRY LaMOTHE**

Inspired by true events

US $14.95 CAN $20.95
ISBN 978-0-9820653-0-3

CASWELL
COMMUNICATIONS

GHETTO GIRLS IV

Young Luv

Ghetto Girls IV Young Luv
$14.95 // 9780979281662

Ghetto Girls
$14.95 // 0975945319

Ghetto Girls Too
$14.95 // 0975945300

Ghetto Girls 3 Soo Hood
$14.95 // 0975945351

THE BEST OF THE STREET CHRONICLES TODAY, THE **GHETTO GIRLS SERIES** IS A WONDERFULLY HYPNOTIC ADVENTURE THAT DELVES INTO THE CONVOLUTED MINDS OF CRIMINALS AND THE DARK WORLD OF POLICE CORRUPTION. YET, THERE IS SOMETHING THRILLING AND SURPRISINGLY TENDER ABOUT THIS ONGOING YOUNG-ADULT SAGA FILLED WITH MAD FLAVA.

Love and a Gangsta
author // **ERICK S GRAY**

This explosive sequel to **Crave All Lose All**. Soul and America were together ten years 'til Soul's incarceration for drugs. Faithfully, she waited four years for his return. Once home they find life ain't so easy anymore. America believes in holding her man down and expects Soul to be as committed. His lust for fast money rears its ugly head at the same time America's music career takes off. From shootouts, to hustling and thugging life, Soul and his man, Omega, have done it. Omega is on the come-up in the drug-game of South Jamaica, Queens. Using ties to a Mexican drug cartel, Omega has Queens in his grip. His older brother, Rahmel, was Soul's cellmate in an upstate prison. Rahmel, a man of God, tries to counsel Soul. Omega introduces New York to crystal meth. Misery loves company and on the road to the riches and spoils of the game, Omega wants the only man he can trust, Soul, with him. Love between Soul and America is tested by an unforgivable greed that leads quickly to deception and murder.

$14.95 // 9780979281648

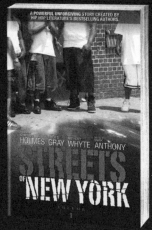  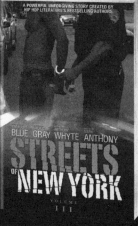

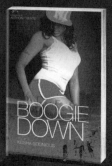